Trouble strikes
at the Great Wall!

The cable car to take them up to the Great Wall pulled onto the platform, and the attendant directed the children inside. Jessie, Benny, and Violet were already in when someone behind Henry yelled "Watch out!" in a scared voice. Henry stumbled forward into the car, but a person outside the car reached in and took hold of the strap on the duffel bag. Henry tried to grab it back, but the bag was yanked off Henry's shoulder as the door closed. "Wait!" Henry yelled, but the car was already moving away from the station. The duffel bag was gone...

THE BOXCAR CHILDREN
SURPRISE ISLAND
THE YELLOW HOUSE MYSTERY
MYSTERY RANCH
MIKE'S MYSTERY
BLUE BAY MYSTERY
THE WOODSHED MYSTERY
THE LIGHTHOUSE MYSTERY
MOUNTAIN TOP MYSTERY
SCHOOLHOUSE MYSTERY
CABOOSE MYSTERY
HOUSEBOAT MYSTERY
SNOWBOUND MYSTERY
TREE HOUSE MYSTERY
BICYCLE MYSTERY
MYSTERY IN THE SAND
MYSTERY BEHIND THE WALL
BUS STATION MYSTERY
BENNY UNCOVERS A MYSTERY
THE HAUNTED CABIN MYSTERY
THE DESERTED LIBRARY MYSTERY
THE ANIMAL SHELTER MYSTERY
THE OLD MOTEL MYSTERY
THE MYSTERY OF THE HIDDEN PAINTING
THE AMUSEMENT PARK MYSTERY
THE MYSTERY OF THE MIXED-UP ZOO
THE CAMP-OUT MYSTERY
THE MYSTERY GIRL
THE MYSTERY CRUISE
THE DISAPPEARING FRIEND MYSTERY
THE MYSTERY OF THE SINGING GHOST
THE MYSTERY IN THE SNOW
THE PIZZA MYSTERY
THE MYSTERY HORSE
THE MYSTERY AT THE DOG SHOW
THE CASTLE MYSTERY
THE MYSTERY OF THE LOST VILLAGE
THE MYSTERY ON THE ICE
THE MYSTERY OF THE PURPLE POOL
THE GHOST SHIP MYSTERY
THE MYSTERY IN WASHINGTON, DC
THE CANOE TRIP MYSTERY
THE MYSTERY OF THE HIDDEN BEACH
THE MYSTERY OF THE MISSING CAT
THE MYSTERY AT SNOWFLAKE INN

THE MYSTERY ON STAGE
THE DINOSAUR MYSTERY
THE MYSTERY OF THE STOLEN MUSIC
THE MYSTERY AT THE BALL PARK
THE CHOCOLATE SUNDAE MYSTERY
THE MYSTERY OF THE HOT AIR BALLOON
THE MYSTERY BOOKSTORE
THE PILGRIM VILLAGE MYSTERY
THE MYSTERY OF THE STOLEN BOXCAR
THE MYSTERY IN THE CAVE
THE MYSTERY ON THE TRAIN
THE MYSTERY AT THE FAIR
THE MYSTERY OF THE LOST MINE
THE GUIDE DOG MYSTERY
THE HURRICANE MYSTERY
THE PET SHOP MYSTERY
THE MYSTERY OF THE SECRET MESSAGE
THE FIREHOUSE MYSTERY
THE MYSTERY IN SAN FRANCISCO
THE NIAGARA FALLS MYSTERY
THE MYSTERY AT THE ALAMO
THE OUTER SPACE MYSTERY
THE SOCCER MYSTERY
THE MYSTERY IN THE OLD ATTIC
THE GROWLING BEAR MYSTERY
THE MYSTERY OF THE LAKE MONSTER
THE MYSTERY AT PEACOCK HALL
THE WINDY CITY MYSTERY
THE BLACK PEARL MYSTERY
THE CEREAL BOX MYSTERY
THE PANTHER MYSTERY
THE MYSTERY OF THE QUEEN'S JEWELS
THE STOLEN SWORD MYSTERY
THE BASKETBALL MYSTERY
THE MOVIE STAR MYSTERY
THE MYSTERY OF THE PIRATE'S MAP
THE GHOST TOWN MYSTERY
THE MYSTERY OF THE BLACK RAVEN
THE MYSTERY IN THE MALL
THE MYSTERY IN NEW YORK
THE GYMNASTICS MYSTERY
THE POISON FROG MYSTERY
THE MYSTERY OF THE EMPTY SAFE
THE HOME RUN MYSTERY
THE GREAT BICYCLE RACE MYSTERY

THE MYSTERY OF THE WILD PONIES
THE MYSTERY IN THE COMPUTER GAME
THE HONEYBEE MYSTERY
THE MYSTERY AT THE CROOKED HOUSE
THE HOCKEY MYSTERY
THE MYSTERY OF THE MIDNIGHT DOG
THE MYSTERY OF THE SCREECH OWL
THE SUMMER CAMP MYSTERY
THE COPYCAT MYSTERY
THE HAUNTED CLOCK TOWER MYSTERY
THE MYSTERY OF THE TIGER'S EYE
THE DISAPPEARING STAIRCASE MYSTERY
THE MYSTERY ON BLIZZARD MOUNTAIN
THE MYSTERY OF THE SPIDER'S CLUE
THE CANDY FACTORY MYSTERY
THE MYSTERY OF THE MUMMY'S CURSE
THE MYSTERY OF THE STAR RUBY
THE STUFFED BEAR MYSTERY
THE MYSTERY OF ALLIGATOR SWAMP
THE MYSTERY AT SKELETON POINT
THE TATTLETALE MYSTERY
THE COMIC BOOK MYSTERY
THE GREAT SHARK MYSTERY
THE ICE CREAM MYSTERY
THE MIDNIGHT MYSTERY
THE MYSTERY IN THE FORTUNE COOKIE
THE BLACK WIDOW SPIDER MYSTERY
THE RADIO MYSTERY
THE MYSTERY OF THE RUNAWAY GHOST
THE FINDERS KEEPERS MYSTERY
THE MYSTERY OF THE HAUNTED BOXCAR
THE CLUE IN THE CORN MAZE
THE GHOST OF THE CHATTERING BONES
THE SWORD OF THE SILVER KNIGHT
THE GAME STORE MYSTERY
THE MYSTERY OF THE ORPHAN TRAIN
THE VANISHING PASSENGER
THE GIANT YO-YO MYSTERY
THE CREATURE IN OGOPOGO LAKE
THE ROCK 'N' ROLL MYSTERY
THE SECRET OF THE MASK
THE SEATTLE PUZZLE
THE GHOST IN THE FIRST ROW
THE BOX THAT WATCH FOUND
A HORSE NAMED DRAGON

THE GREAT DETECTIVE RACE
THE GHOST AT THE DRIVE-IN MOVIE
THE MYSTERY OF THE TRAVELING TOMATOES
THE SPY GAME
THE DOG-GONE MYSTERY
THE VAMPIRE MYSTERY
SUPERSTAR WATCH
THE SPY IN THE BLEACHERS
THE AMAZING MYSTERY SHOW
THE PUMPKIN HEAD MYSTERY
THE CUPCAKE CAPER
THE CLUE IN THE RECYCLING BIN
MONKEY TROUBLE
THE ZOMBIE PROJECT
THE GREAT TURKEY HEIST
THE GARDEN THIEF
THE BOARDWALK MYSTERY
THE MYSTERY OF THE FALLEN TREASURE
THE RETURN OF THE GRAVEYARD GHOST
THE MYSTERY OF THE STOLEN SNOWBOARD
THE MYSTERY OF THE WILD WEST BANDIT
THE MYSTERY OF THE GRINNING GARGOYLE
THE MYSTERY OF THE SOCCER SNITCH
THE MYSTERY OF THE MISSING POP IDOL
THE MYSTERY OF THE STOLEN DINOSAUR BONES
THE MYSTERY AT THE CALGARY STAMPEDE
THE SLEEPY HOLLOW MYSTERY
THE LEGEND OF THE IRISH CASTLE
THE CELEBRITY CAT CAPER
HIDDEN IN THE HAUNTED SCHOOL
THE ELECTION DAY DILEMMA
JOURNEY ON A RUNAWAY TRAIN
THE CLUE IN THE PAPYRUS SCROLL
THE DETOUR OF THE ELEPHANTS
THE SHACKLETON SABOTAGE
THE KHIPU AND THE FINAL KEY

THE BOXCAR CHILDREN ®

CREATED BY
GERTRUDE CHANDLER WARNER

GREAT **3** ADVENTURE

THE DETOUR OF THE ELEPHANTS

STORY BY
DEE GARRETSON AND JM LEE

ILLUSTRATED BY
ANTHONY VANARSDALE

ALBERT WHITMAN & COMPANY
CHICAGO, ILLINOIS

Contents

Flight to the Far East

"I wish we could have stayed longer in Italy," ten-year-old Violet Alden said as she watched the streets of Rome flash by from the window of the car.

"I know," Violet's older brother Henry said. "But if there is a bad storm coming, we need to get to the plane right away." Henry, who was fourteen, had received a call from the copilot of the private jet they had been traveling on. Emilio told them to hurry to the airport, because if they didn't take off soon, they might have to stay in Rome for several days. A late-spring ice storm was bearing down on the city. "We'll come back to Rome someday when we can spend more time here. The Reddimus Society is counting on us

1

to deliver the rest of the artifacts safely and as quickly as possible."

A secret society had recruited the Alden children to return stolen art and artifacts to their rightful owners. When the head of the society, Mrs. Silverton, had asked the Aldens to help, she hadn't realized a family of thieves, the Argents, would be trying to get the artifacts away from the children before they could be delivered.

"Yes," twelve-year-old Jessie said. "We'll come back when we don't have to worry about the Argents following us." She was worried because they still had four artifacts left and didn't yet know where to deliver them. With each artifact, they had received clues to help them find its destination. They had already been to New Mexico to deliver a Native American piece of pottery, Egypt to return a valuable figurine of an Egyptian pharaoh, and England to deliver a small gold piece of jewelry from the time Stonehenge was built.

"We'll be back," Benny, the youngest Alden said, "because we threw the coins in the fountain." Mrs. McGregor had told them about the legend that if a person threw a coin in the Trevi Fountain, that person would come back to Rome. Benny, who was six, had a lot of fun at the fountain. "I wish I knew where we are going now though," Benny added, sighing. "I like the plane a lot, but we can't just fly around in circles. And I wish Mrs. McGregor were coming with us." Their housekeeper, Mrs. McGregor, had been with them in England and Italy. Benny was sad when she said good-bye to them as they got in the car.

"Remember she promised there will be other people to help us at our next stops," Jessie told him. "Besides, Mrs. McGregor needs to get home. I'm sure Grandfather misses her." The Aldens lived with their grandfather. After their parents had died, the Aldens ran away, afraid their grandfather would be mean. They lived in an old boxcar in the woods until he found them and they discovered he wasn't the least bit mean. He even moved the boxcar to the backyard of his house so they could play in it whenever they wanted.

"Watch must be missing her too," Violet said. "Without us there, Watch will be lonely." Watch was the Aldens' dog. Sometimes he got to go with them on their adventures, but this time it wouldn't have been easy to take him along.

Jessie picked up the package they had received at their hotel right before Emilio called. They had opened it there but hadn't had a chance to work out what the clues meant. "Don't worry, Benny. The answer to our next destination is in here. We just have to figure out what the clues mean. Once we are on the plane, we'll work on it."

The driver took them to the terminal where the private planes were parked. Then an airport official escorted the children out to their plane, where Emilio was waiting at the top of the steps.

He waved when he saw them. "All aboard!" he yelled. It began to rain just as they went up the steps. The rain was very cold.

The pilot, Mr. Ganert, came out of the cockpit. "The front edge of the storm is already here, but we can't take off until we know where we are going," Mr. Ganert said. "I need to file a flight plan. You Aldens are supposed to be so clever; let's hear the plan."

"We're working on it," Jessie said, opening up the package once more. She took out the red silk bag with a gold design on it that held the clues.

Mr. Ganert frowned at the sight of the bag. None of the children liked Mr. Ganert. He was a good pilot, but he was not very friendly. He hadn't wanted the Aldens to be in charge of the artifacts, and they knew he didn't trust them to keep the items safe.

"Well, hurry up," Mr. Ganert grumbled as he went back into the cockpit.

Jessie opened the bag and took out the clues, which were some wooden stamps, an ink pad, and an envelope with a riddle inside. The envelope had a little drawing of an owl on it. Reddimus Society agents used the owl on their messages because owls moved quietly and without anyone noticing, just like the agents tried to do.

Six of the seven wooden stamps had letters on them. Benny picked up the one without a letter. It pictured a dragon instead. "A country of many dragons? Dragons aren't real. I wish they were. I'd like to go to a country full of dragons."

Violet looked over Benny's shoulder to get a

better look at the stamp. "This dragon doesn't have wings. Pictures I've seen of dragons show them with wings."

"It's really long and skinny too," Benny said. "It almost looks like a snake with legs and arms."

Jessie handed Henry the envelope. "I'll get my laptop going. If this riddle is like the others, we are going to have to research parts of it. Would you read it out loud again?"

Henry took out the riddle and started to read.

> *You are going to need to be very, very clever.*
> *There will be riddles here, riddles there,*
> > *riddles everywhere.*
> *The path grows more twisted to confuse those*
> > *who follow you.*

He looked up. "That part means the Argents. It sounds as if we will have to solve more riddles than before to find the place to deliver the next artifact."

"I hope we can do it," Violet said. "The riddles have been hard."

"We'll manage," Henry said. He kept reading.

The Detour of the Elephants

Something that changed the world started with
    blocks like these,
Though the symbols carved on them few could
    read today.
To have books, you must first have a way to
    make words.
Handwriting is good, but to spread words far
    and wide, something more is needed.
Figure out what these blocks do and where they
    first were made,
And you will find your next destination—a city
    where the dragons ruled.

Violet picked up the ink pad and one of the stamps. "We can stamp letters with these and make words. I don't understand the invention part. Is it where wooden stamps were invented?"

"I think I get it," Henry said. He read part of the riddle again. *"To have books, you must first have a way to make words.*

"It's printing. Wooden stamps like these were the way things like scrolls and then books were first printed. Later on, the stamps were made of

8

metal, and then the printing press was invented, but it all started with these stamps."

"Henry is right. We need to find out where printing was invented," Jessie said. She typed a question into her laptop. "It's China!" she announced. "Printing was invented in China."

"We're going to China!" Henry called to Emilio and Mr. Ganert.

They came out of the cockpit. "Are you sure?" Mr. Ganert asked. "That is a long way. I had hoped we were going somewhere closer."

"We're sure," Jessie said.

Mr. Ganert sighed. "I'll start on a flight plan. You'd better figure out which city in China. It's a big country." A gust of wind shook the plane. "And you'd better figure it out fast," he called over his shoulder as he went back into the cockpit.

"It's going to be hard to figure out," Henry said. "There are thousands of cities and towns in China. It's a big country, like Mr. Ganert said. It's about the same size as the United States."

"I'm sure you can do it," Emilio said. "I suppose I'd better go help with the flight plan." He went back to the cockpit.

"We have a *C*, a *J*, an *E*, an *I*, a *G*, an *N*, an *A*, an *H*, and a *B*," Benny said, looking at each stamp.

"We know we're going to China. We can spell that out." Violet sorted the letters, taking out the ones for *China* and stamping the word on a piece of paper. "That leaves *J*, *G*, *E*, and *B*," she said as she stamped those letters one by one on another piece of paper.

"That isn't much of a clue," Henry said. "There is only one vowel. Jessie, can you find a list of Chinese cities on your laptop?"

They tried all different combinations of the letters but couldn't find any cities that matched. The wind grew stronger, and they could hear pellets of icy rain pinging on the airplane.

Benny picked up the stamp with the *N* on it. "This stamp is scratched," he said. "It has two little marks in one corner." His siblings weren't paying attention. They had gone back to reading the riddle.

"The riddle said something about a city where the dragons ruled. What does that mean?" Violet asked.

"Let me see if I can figure it out," Jessie said, going back to her laptop.

Benny looked at the other stamps. The *I* had three scratches on it, but the others didn't have any.

"I found something," Jessie said. "China used to be ruled by emperors, and some emperors thought they descended from dragons. The emperors lived in Beijing, and that's the capital of China. That could be the city where the dragons ruled."

"How do you spell Beijing?" Benny asked. "Do these letters help spell it?" He pushed the two stamps with the scratches on them toward Jessie. "They have scratches on them. What if we use the *N* two times and the *I* three times? My name has two Ns in it. I would use the same stamp twice to spell my name."

"Benny, that's so smart!" Jessie said. "You're right. We can use each stamp more than once. That's what they'd have to do when they were printing in the old days. They wouldn't have had lots of stamps for the same letter." She moved the stamps around. "Yes, they do spell Beijing. We're going to the capital city of China!"

Emilio came out of the cockpit, and the children told him their destination.

"I'll let the Reddimus Society know so they can make arrangements for someone to meet you when we land," Emilio said. Mrs. Silverton's granddaughter, Trudy, handled all the arrangements for their travel from her office at the Reddimus Society headquarters. She was very good at making sure the Aldens managed to get to everywhere they needed to go. And once they had arrived at a destination, she made sure they had places to stay and people to drive them around.

"We'll have to stop partway to get the right paperwork to go to China," Emilio added, "and for fuel and some sleep, so buckle up and settle in."

"I'm excited to go to China," Violet said. "The Argents won't be able to follow us there. They won't know where we've gone."

"I hope not," Jessie said, "though they did manage to follow us to our other stops."

Emilio and Mr. Ganert took turns flying the plane. Mr. Ganert never talked to them. When he wasn't flying, he went to a seat right behind the cockpit and napped. Benny thought Mr. Ganert had a mean look on his face even when he was sleeping.

Violet played with the wooden stamps, trying to see how many words she could make. Emilio came out of the cockpit, sat down, and picked up the dragon stamp. "Nice," he said. "Say, would you like to hear a joke?"

Jessie knew even if they said no, he'd tell one anyway. Emilio loved jokes, and the sillier the joke, the better. Benny thought they were all funny.

"What do peas and dragons have in common?" Emilio asked. He had a grin on his face.

Benny thought for moment. "I don't know. Are they both green?"

Emilio's grin grew bigger. "Good answer, but that's not the one I'm thinking of. Peas and dragons are alike because you can't balance either one on a fork!" Emilio burst out laughing. He always laughed at his own jokes.

Everyone else laughed too, mainly because it was funny to see Emilio so excited about his joke.

They read, played games, and watched a movie on the flight. Emilio came out of the cockpit at different points to help them make meals and to talk. The plane had a small galley in the back stocked with all sorts of good food and snacks. After several hours, they landed in a country called Kazakhstan to collect the paperwork they needed and so the pilots could rest. They spent the night in a hotel at the airport, leaving very early the next morning.

The rest of the flight was bumpy and not very much fun. Everyone buckled their seat belts and sat back to watch another movie to take their minds off the rough air. When the plane rose up and then moved down all of the sudden, a bowl of popcorn on the table tipped over and some of the popcorn spilled out. They waited until Mr. Ganert said they could move around again before they cleaned up the mess.

Emilio helped them. "Even spilled popcorn has a use," he said. "Would you like to see a game?"

"Sure!" Benny said.

"Jessie, there are some small red plastic cups in the galley. Would you get them?" Emilio asked.

Jessie brought Emilio the cups. He set them out on the table upside down. "This is called a shell game. It's a good game to practice your skills at observing," he told them. "Reddimus agents have to stay sharp, so anything you can do to practice helps. The shell game is very old. Some people think it first became popular in ancient Greece. But they didn't play it with cups and popcorn. They probably used nut shells and dried peas."

"I've seen this," Henry said. "It's called sleight of hand."

"That's right," Emilio said.

"What does that mean?" Benny asked.

"*Sleight* can mean to trick someone by being good at moving your hands very quickly," Henry explained. "It's what magicians do with a lot of their tricks."

"Yes," Emilio said. "That's how many of them start out. You start this trick by putting an object under the middle cup." He lifted up the cup and put a piece of popcorn under it. "Now, pay attention. See if you can keep track of where it goes." He slid the cups into different positions so fast it was hard to keep track of them. Then he did it several more times, each time moving the cups very quickly.

"I lost track," Jessie said.

"Me too," Henry said.

"I think it's under that one." Benny pointed at the one on the right.

"No, it's back under the middle one," Violet said. "I'm sure of it."

Emilio picked up the cup on the right. There was nothing under it. He picked up the one on the left. There was nothing under that one either. His hand hovered over the middle cup.

"It's under there!" Violet said. "I was watching it."

Emilio picked up the cup. The piece of popcorn was back where it had started.

"Good job, Violet," Henry said.

"Now I'll do it again." Emilio moved the cups closer to the edge of the table and started the trick again. When he was finished, all the Aldens were sure the popcorn was under the cup on the left. Emilio picked up that cup. Nothing was there. "See which one it's under, Benny."

Benny picked up the other two. There was no popcorn! "Where did it go?" Benny cried.

Emilio bent down and picked up the piece of

popcorn off the floor. "I moved the cups closer to the edge of the table so I could slide it all the way off. The audience is convinced it has to be under one of the cups. They don't think about looking for it somewhere else."

"That's a good trick!" Violet said.

"It is," Henry said. It gave him the beginning of an idea. He sat back to ponder.

By the time the plane was ready to land in Beijing, everyone was ready to get off and start the next part of their mission. Once the plane had landed and arrived at an airport gate, Emilio came out of the cockpit. "I've talked to Mrs. Silverton. You are in for a surprise," he said.

"Are you going to tell us what it is?" Violet asked.

Emilio smiled. "No, you will have to wait." He looked out one of the windows. "Trudy has arranged for a man named Mr. Shen who works at the airport to take you to get your passports checked and to direct you to the main terminal. I see a man waiting. I'm sure that's him."

They collected all their things and went down the plane's staircase to meet Mr. Shen.

The Detour of the Elephants

He greeted them and took them into the terminal. After they were through the customs line, Mr. Shen said, "We are meeting the rest of your party in the Imperial Garden Pavilion. Come this way, please."

"Who is the rest of our party?" Jessie asked.

"I'm sorry, I don't know their names," Mr. Shen said. "You will see them very soon."

"There is a garden inside the airport?" Henry asked.

"Yes," Mr. Shen replied, "it is built to look like one of the gardens at the Imperial Palace. Of course, it is much smaller. It's right over here."

"There are buildings inside this building!" Benny said. "Except they don't have any walls." Ahead of them were some small buildings with roofs held up by red pillars. The buildings were surrounded by rocks and looked out over a small pond.

"The buildings are called pavilions," Mr. Shen explained. "I see the members of your party." Three people stood in one of the pavilions waving at them.

2

A Riddle over Dumplings

Benny saw them first. "It's Cousin Alice and Cousin Joe and Soo Lee!" he cried. He was very excited to see Soo Lee. She was the same age as he was, and they had been good friends ever since Cousin Joe and Cousin Alice had adopted her from Korea.

Cousin Alice hugged all of them when they got to the pavilion, and she thanked Mr. Shen for bringing them. After Mr. Shen said good-bye, Cousin Joe said, "We arrived just a little while ago. We have been all packed for a few days and were just waiting for a call from the Silvertons about your next destination. They made all the arrangements for us."

"We got to fly on a really big plane where the

seats got turned into beds!" Soo Lee told them. "It was really fun."

"How did you get here before us?" Violet asked. "China is a long way from Connecticut, isn't it?"

"It is," Cousin Alice said. "But the planes take what you could call a shortcut. They fly right over the North Pole, so it isn't as far as you think."

"And remember, we stopped halfway and spent the night," Henry said. "They didn't have to stop."

"You arrived just at the right time. We're so glad you're here," Jessie said.

"It sounds like you have had a very exciting time," Cousin Alice said, hugging Benny again.

"I hope we get to have more exciting times now that we're here too," Soo Lee said.

"What's this I hear about one of the Silvertons who has gone missing?" Cousin Joe asked. "We heard the FBI thinks she's been stealing items instead of returning them."

"We don't believe it," Henry said. "It's Tricia Silverton, who is Trudy's sister. She was seen in Paris at the same time a valuable ring was stolen, but we don't think she took it. She's been leaving us clues to where we are supposed to deliver the artifacts."

"It doesn't make sense that Tricia would be stealing art and jewelry at the same time she is helping us return valuable things," Jessie said. "We've been in contact with Mr. Carter from the FBI about our latest clues. We are supposed to contact him when we get more." The Aldens had first met Mr. Carter back when he helped investigate a mystery at their aunt's ranch. They had been surprised to learn he was investigating some recent art and jewelry thefts in Europe and Africa.

"I don't understand why she doesn't just call you and explain where you are supposed to go," Cousin Joe said.

"We don't understand it either," Violet said. "It's a big mystery."

"We just know she's not a bad person," Benny added.

"I hope it all gets straightened out soon," Cousin Alice said. "I don't know where we are going now that we are in Beijing, but the Silvertons arranged a driver for us. She won't be here for another hour.

They thought you wouldn't be arriving until a little later."

"Good," Henry said. "We need some time before we leave the airport to figure out a better way to keep the artifacts safe." He told Cousin Joe, Cousin Alice, and Soo Lee about the attempt to steal the duffel bag in Egypt. "I have an idea," he continued. "The Argents know the artifacts are in the duffel bag. So they aren't safe there anymore. We need to move them into something else, but we don't want the Argents to know exactly where they are. I had an idea we could do something like the shell game Emilio showed us." He explained Emilio's trick and then continued. "If we divide up the artifacts into other bags but still carry the duffel bag, the Argents will think the artifacts are still in there. If they try to steal the artifacts again, they'll try to take the duffel bag. It will be like a decoy."

"That's a good idea," Jessie said. "There are four boxes left. We can each carry one."

"We could put them with our clothes in our backpacks," Violet suggested.

"We could, but I had another idea," Henry said.

22

"We don't want to carry our heavy backpacks with us all the time."

"Where will we put them?" Benny asked.

"We need to look like tourists, and tourists often carry cameras. We can get camera cases. We'll get them for Cousin Alice, Cousin Joe, and Soo Lee too. Their cases will be empty, but no one will know. Even if the Argents figure out the artifacts aren't in the duffel bag, they won't know exactly where they are."

"Mine just might have a real camera in it," Cousin Joe said. He pulled a camera out of another bag. "I've been meaning to get a case for it."

"Where can we get camera cases?" Benny asked.

"Large airports usually have a big variety of stores," Cousin Alice said, "especially for items that tourists want to buy, like cameras. Let's ask at the information desk."

In the camera store, they picked out seven identical camera cases. Jessie asked if they had any small empty boxes they didn't need anymore. The owner found boxes that were almost exactly the same size as the artifact boxes. They thanked the store owner. Then they went back to the terminal and found a quiet spot to sit down.

When Jessie pulled a wooden box out of the duffel bag, Cousin Joe said, "That doesn't look like a safe way to carry a valuable artifact." Cousin Joe and Cousin Alice both loved studying and preserving historical objects.

"It's not supposed to look like there is anything special in it." She opened the lid of the box so Cousin Joe could see the case inside. "The artifact is inside this plastic case. It's all padded inside and, see, there is a keypad lock on it. We don't know the combinations. Each time we go somewhere to deliver an artifact, we're given a riddle and we have to figure it out to get the code."

"That makes more sense," Cousin Alice said. "I was wondering how you were keeping the artifacts from getting damaged."

They divided up the remaining artifacts and then took the paper they'd taken off the wooden boxes and wrapped the pieces around the empty cardboard boxes. "Maybe we can get some tape at our next hotel," Jessie said. "But for now this is good enough. We may not run into any Argents at all."

"I hope not," Violet said. "I'd be happy if I never saw the Argents again."

Cousin Joe checked his watch. "It's time to meet the driver. She is supposed to be right outside Exit B with a blue van. She'll have a sign that says Aldens on it."

They easily found the driver. She was a young woman who introduced herself as Mary Burke. When she greeted them, she spoke with an American accent that sounded like she was from the South. "Hello there," she said. "Welcome to Beijing!"

Once they were in the van, Mary kept up a steady stream of chatter, telling them all about how she had come to China to study art and then had stayed after she got married. "I'm so glad you are able to visit the city. I wish you had time for me to show you all the historical sites and beautiful gardens, but I understand you have important work to do. I've been given an address where I am to take you." She smiled. "Do you like dumplings?"

"We love dumplings," Henry replied.

"Yes," Benny said. "And we think much better when we aren't hungry."

"Wonderful. I was informed I should take you to Mr. Li's Dumpling restaurant. There are many dumpling restaurants in Beijing, but Mr. Li's is popular with some foreign visitors. You can watch dumplings being made there. They are also very good."

"I'd like that," Jessie said. "I've tried to make them, but I'm not very good at it."

As they drove to the restaurant, Violet noticed how many people were on bicycles. When she said she was surprised to see so many, Mary explained, "It's an easy way to get around. You don't get stuck in so many traffic jams."

Mary pulled up in front of a restaurant. She handed Jessie a card with a phone number written on it. "Call me when you are ready for more rides. The lady who hired me, Mrs. Silverton, paid me to drive you anywhere you want for the next few days. You can leave whatever luggage you want in the van. Enjoy your meal."

They left their backpacks but took the camera

bags and the duffel bag and got out of the car.

"I can already smell the dumplings!" Benny said. He could hardly wait to try them.

The door to the restaurant had bells on it that jingled when Cousin Alice opened the door. The restaurant wasn't very big, but it was crowded with people. Long tables filled the room and colorful travel posters covered the walls. Red paper lanterns hung from the ceiling. At the back of the restaurant, two women were busy filling the dumpling wrappers and sealing them shut, then passing them on to be cooked in large pans.

A man came up to them. "Welcome to our restaurant. You must be the Aldens. I am Mr. Li. We've been expecting you." He showed them to a table, and after they were seated, he said, "I'm afraid my daughter was supposed to be here to meet you, but she telephoned to say she'd be late. While you are waiting for her, if you'd like, I'll bring you an assortment of dumplings so you can taste several kinds."

"Yes, that would be terrific," Jessie said. "Thank you. Can we watch the cooks make the dumplings?"

"Of course," Mr. Li said. "Many visitors like to do that."

The children joined the other customers who were gathered in front of the preparation and cooking stations. The cooks worked very quickly.

"I'm going to practice more when I get home," Jessie said. "I don't know if I'll ever be that fast though!"

When the dumplings were ready, they went back to their table, and a waitress brought the Aldens a big platter of dumplings. Everyone was so hungry it didn't take long for the dumplings to disappear.

"Jessie, when we get home, you have to practice a lot," Benny said. "I could eat these every day."

"Me too!" Soo Lee said. "I'll help you practice too."

Jessie laughed. "That will be fun," she said.

Mr. Li came back to their table. "My daughter called again. She will be here soon, and she asked me to give you this." He handed Henry an envelope and then went to greet some other customers.

The envelope had a tiny drawing of an owl on it. Henry opened it. "It's another riddle. Wait, there's a second page. There are two riddles. Both of them have owl symbols on them."

"Why owls?" Soo Lee asked.

Violet explained about the Reddimus Society logo and then asked Henry, "What does the first page say?"

Henry read it out loud:

> *I am a very large dragon.*
> *My tail winds through miles and miles of*
>   *mountains, deserts, and grasslands.*
> *I protected my people from those in the North.*
> *Now in peace you may walk upon my back and*
>   *gaze out in wonder.*
> *If you can find out when I stopped growing, you*
>   *will see one of my treasures.*

"There's something else." Henry turned the paper so they could see. In big black letters at the bottom of the page were the words, *DON'T SHOW THE ARTIFACT TO ANYONE UNTIL YOU CAN DELIVER IT. KEEP IT SAFE.* There was one more line in smaller letters: *If you need a clue, there is one right near you.*

Violet shivered. "I'm worried we can't keep the artifacts safe." She looked around the restaurant. "What if some of these people work for the Argents?"

"I don't think so," Jessie said. "I don't know how the Argents would find out we were coming to this restaurant. I don't know how they'd even find out we've come to China."

"Should I read the second riddle?" Henry asked.

"No, let's work on one at a time," Jessie said.

Henry read it again.

"How could you walk on a dragon's back?" Benny asked. "Even if dragons were real, I don't think they'd like it if you walked on them."

"We know dragons aren't real, so maybe it's something like a statue of a dragon. We could walk on the back of that," Violet suggested.

"But a statue couldn't be miles and miles long," Jessie said.

"Does this riddle make sense to either of you?" Henry asked Cousin Alice and Cousin Joe.

Cousin Joe shook his head. "I can't make heads or tails of it."

"I can't either," Cousin Alice said.

Violet tried to think about the riddle, but she was distracted by all the posters on the walls. She got up to look more closely at them. There was one of some pretty gardens, and one of some boats on a river. Another showed a big wall winding across the tops of some mountains. As she stared at it, she noticed the words on the poster.

Printed at the bottom it said, Tour the great Earth Dragon of China. She stared at it and then said, "I found something. Come look."

The rest of the Aldens joined her. Benny looked up at the poster. "That is a gigantic wall."

"It's the Great Wall of China," Henry said. "We learned about it in school. It was built to protect China from invaders from the North."

Violet pointed. "See the words on the poster? Tour the great Earth Dragon."

A man sitting at a nearby table overheard them. "Yes, Westerners call it the Great Wall, but it has several other names. Some here in China refer to it as 'The Earth Dragon.'"

The Aldens looked at each other, and then Henry said to the man, "Thank you. We didn't know that."

Jessie said to the others, "Let's go back to our table." She thought the man was a regular tourist, but she thought that, to be safe, they shouldn't talk about the riddle where anyone could overhear them.

They sat back down. "That was a good find," Henry said to Violet. He picked up the riddle again. "I think we know what the first and second lines mean now."

> *I am a very large dragon.*
> *My tail winds through miles and miles of*
> *   mountains, deserts, and grasslands.*
> *I protected my people from those in the North.*

"It does look big enough to walk on too," Jessie said. "That fits the next line."

"Yes, it is a very strong, thick wall," Henry said. "It was built so that, in some parts, ten men or five men on horseback could walk side by side."

"I still don't understand the last line," Violet picked up the riddle and read it. *"If you can find out when I stopped growing, you will see one of my treasures."*

"It took a very long time to build," Henry said. "Hundreds and hundreds of years, but at some point they stopped building new sections. Maybe it means when it was finished." Henry pulled out his phone and brought up a website about the Great Wall. "This says it was finished in 1644. See if that's the code for the case."

"Should we open the case here?" Violet looked around at all the other people in the restaurant. No one seemed to be paying attention to them, but she was still worried.

"Let's just take a quick look and then lock it back up," Jessie said. She punched in the code and opened the lid.

Inside the box was a small clay disc. It had a Chinese character carved into it.

"I don't know what this is," Jessie said. "Does anyone have any ideas?"

"No, unless it's a piece of jewelry," Violet suggested. "But I don't see any way to attach it to a necklace or pin it on."

"It looks like a game piece, like a checker," Benny said.

"Benny is right. It does look like a checker," Soo Lee said. "But why is there only one?"

"It's old, whatever it is," Cousin Alice said.

More and more people came into the restaurant. Violet looked at each person carefully. All the people were making her nervous. Any of them could be working for the Argents. "Let's close the lid before anyone sees it," she said.

Henry closed the lid. "Now we just need to figure out where to take this."

3

The Place of Many Puzzles

"Do you think the clue means we get to go to the Great Wall?" Benny asked. "I want to walk on top of it."

"Maybe," Henry told him. "We'd need to know exactly where to go. The information on this website says the Great Wall is more than ten thousand miles long, though the most well-known part is only five thousand five hundred miles long."

"Only!" Cousin Alice exclaimed. "That's almost twice the distance between New York and California."

"Can we hear the other riddle?" Violet asked.

Before Henry could read it, the bells on the door jingled. A young Chinese woman who looked a few years older than Henry came rushing into the restaurant. She was wearing a black beret and was dressed in all black except for a bright red scarf around her neck. She had a big black camera bag slung over her shoulder. Many customers in the restaurant greeted her like they were her friends. She looked around the restaurant. When she saw the Aldens, she waved and made her way around the tables to them.

"Hello," the young woman said. "I'm Wenwen Li. I'm so sorry I'm late. I should have been here when you arrived."

"It's all right," Jessie said. "We had some wonderful dumplings while we waited." Jessie introduced everyone.

Wenwen sat down and said, "Tricia Silverton asked me to help you."

"Is Tricia here in Beijing?" Jessie asked. She thought they might finally be able to figure out what was going on.

"I don't know," Wenwen said. "I received an email from her about you just a few hours ago. It didn't say anything about her being in the city. After that, a messenger delivered the envelopes."

She looked down at the table. "Good, I see my father gave them to you."

"Did Tricia tell you how you were supposed to help us?" Henry asked.

"I act as her guide when she is here in Beijing." Wenwen took the camera bag off her shoulder and set it on the table. "I want to be a travel photographer someday, so right now I travel all over Beijing and take pictures of all sorts of interesting sites. I know the city very well, and it's easier for visitors if they have a guide who speaks Chinese. Tricia didn't say exactly what she wanted me to help you with, but I just assumed she meant for me to be your guide."

"Are you any good at riddles?" Jessie asked. She already felt like they could trust the young woman.

"I love riddles!" Wenwen said.

"Good, because we have one to solve before we can tell a guide where to take us." Henry read the second riddle.

Your path will take you on a visit to the nine dragons near the northern sea.

The Place of Many Puzzles

All are fantastic, but only one will help you
    continue on your quest.
Find a dragon that is the color of the sky right
    before the sun rises.
There are two, but only one is roaring.
Count from the right to find his place in line.
Then find the smallest of streets that matches
    that place.
Your next puzzle awaits you in a place of many
    puzzles.

Wenwen laughed. "I see why Tricia asked me to help. I showed her the spot in the riddle. It's a place called the Nine Dragon Wall in Beihai Park. I can take you there, and then maybe we can figure out the rest of the riddle."

"What's the best way to get there?" Jessie asked.

"There is so much traffic today, it would be easiest to go by bicycle," Wenwen replied. "My bicycle is right outside, and there's a bicycle rental place down the street."

"Fun!" Soo Lee said. "I knew this was going to be a good trip."

The Detour of the Elephants

"I think Cousin Joe and I will go to our hotel while you solve this riddle," Cousin Alice said. "We're tired from traveling. Soo Lee can go with you though."

"Yay!" Soo Lee cried. "I'm not a bit tired."

"We'll see you at the hotel then," Cousin Joe said. "I'll call Mary and tell her you'll call her when you are ready to be picked up. Good luck with the riddle."

Wenwen told Cousin Joe where they were going, and then she took the children to a bicycle rental shop. Soon they were on their way through the busy streets. The park wasn't far from the restaurant. It was very large, full of pathways and food stands and people. There was a lake in the middle of the park with many people in boats.

"What are these pretty trees?" Violet asked as they rode along. Pink flowers were just opening up on the trees lining the paths.

"They are wild plum trees," Wenwen told her. "Many fruit trees grew here when the park was part of the imperial gardens. That was back when China was ruled by emperors and empresses. The Nine Dragon Wall is ahead. See the bright colors?"

The Place of Many Puzzles

They came to halt in front of a long tiled wall with nine vivid dragons on it. Each dragon was bigger than a person. The dragons were like the dragon on the stamp. None of them had wings, and they all had long bodies and tails.

"That is the most beautiful wall I've ever seen," Jessie said with a gasp as they got off their bikes.

"I love all the colors!" Violet cried.

"The dragons are a little scary looking," Benny said.

"Don't be afraid of them," Wenwen told him. "Dragons in China are symbols of strength and good luck. They look fierce because they were supposed to be powerful."

"Look, there are smaller dragons all around the edge too," Soo Lee said.

"Yes, there are supposed to be six hundred and thirty-five dragons total, if you count all the dragons on both sides," Wenwen said. "I've tried to count them, but I always lose track."

"Why was it built?" Henry asked. "Was it a part of a building at one time?"

"No, it was built just like this to stand by itself,"

Wenwen explained. "These kinds of walls screened the entrances to gardens and houses. All of this was part of the imperial gardens. This wall is hundreds of years old. It's about one hundred feet long and twenty feet tall. I've read there is a small copy of this wall in your country, in Chicago. Have you ever seen it?"

"No," Jessie said. "I've never heard of it, but now that I know it's there, I'd like to see it."

"You'll have to come visit us and we can all go see it," Violet suggested.

"Yes, and you can take pictures of it," Benny added.

"I may do that," Wenwen said. "I'd love to take pictures all over the United States."

"These dragons look like they are swimming," Soo Lee said. Some of the tiles showed waves underneath the dragons.

"They are swimming," Wenwen said. "Chinese dragons were thought to have control over all types of water: rain, lakes, rivers, and oceans. That's why I think they are often shown with pearls, because pearls are found in the ocean." She pointed at some large white pearls on the tiles.

The Place of Many Puzzles

Henry pulled the riddle out of his pocket. "I'm glad we got to see this, but it's only the first part of the riddle." He read the next part:

> Find a dragon that is the color of the sky right
> before the sun rises.
> There are two, but only one is roaring.
> Count from the right to find his place in line.

"The color of the sky before the sun rises is black, isn't it?" Benny asked.

"Yes, it's nighttime then," Soo Lee added.

"There's no black dragon," Violet said.

"The sky right before dawn isn't really black," Jessie said. "Don't you remember when we've walked to school in the wintertime? It's more like a dark blue."

Henry smiled. "I see two blue dragons." Both blue dragons were near the center of the wall, on either side of the middle dragon, a bright yellow one.

"Another part solved!" Wenwen exclaimed. "This riddle is fun."

"We know there are two blue dragons, but then

the riddle says to find the one that is roaring," Henry said.

"They don't really roar, do they?" Benny asked, taking a step back.

"No," Jessie said. "Look, one has its mouth open like it could be roaring. The other one has its mouth closed."

"Yes, that has to be it," Henry agreed. "The one with the open mouth looks like it is roaring. The next line says, *Count from the right to find his place in line.*"

Violet counted. "The roaring blue dragon is fourth from the right."

"The next line of the riddle is confusing," Henry said. "*Then find the smallest of streets that matches that place.*"

"I suppose that means something has to match the word *fourth*, but I don't understand the *smallest of streets*. What is the smallest of streets?" Violet asked.

"A lane?" Jessie suggested. "Or a path, but that's not exactly a street."

"How about an alley?" Henry said.

"That's it!" Wenwen cried. "There is a street near here named Fourth Alley."

"What about the last line?" Benny asked.

"*Your next puzzle awaits you in a place of many puzzles*," Henry read. "Do you know what that means?" he asked Wenwen.

"I don't, but once we are there, we may figure it out."

They hopped back on their bikes and followed Wenwen to Fourth Alley. The street was full of shops, restaurants, and coffee shops. They got off their bikes and strolled down the street trying to figure out what the last line of the riddle meant.

Nothing seemed to fit until Benny stopped in front of one small shop. "Is this a toy store?" he asked. The windows of the shop were full of small colorful toy animals made of cloth and some wooden items that looked like blocks glued together. Violet wondered what animal the toys were supposed to be. They had tails and ears and were very cute, but she wasn't quite sure if they were cats or something else.

"You've found it, Benny!" Wenwen said. "This

isn't exactly a toy store. It's a puzzle store." She translated the sign on the front. "It says Three Tigers Puzzles. The wooden pieces in the window are called wood knots. You take them apart and try to put them back together the same way."

"Wenwen is right," Henry said. *"Your next puzzle awaits you in a place of many puzzles."*

They walked into the shop. It was packed with games and puzzles of all sorts. There were also shelves full of the same type of cloth animals they had seen in the window. An older man was behind a counter. He was busy unpacking a box of more wood knots.

Wenwen spoke to the man in Chinese. He replied in English, nodding his head at the Aldens. "Welcome to my store," he said. "I am Mr. Yao."

"Do you know anything about owls?" Benny blurted out.

Mr. Yao smiled. "I do not, but I welcome to my store anyone who does." He pulled a package off a shelf behind him and laid it down on top of the counter. "I have a package here for a group of young Americans who may be inquiring about owls."

"That's us!" Violet said.

"Why don't you go ahead and open it?" Jessie said to Violet.

Violet ripped off the wrapping. Out tumbled some wooden shapes and a sealed envelope with an owl on it. Benny counted the shapes. There were seven of them. "I know all these are triangles and here is a square, but what's this one?" He picked up the piece. "It's like a rectangle, but not exactly."

"It's a parallelogram," Jessie said.

Soo Lee picked up another piece. "There's writing in Chinese on this one."

"This one too," Henry said. When they looked over all the pieces, they realized there were Chinese characters on both sides of each piece.

"It's most unusual," Mr. Yao said. "I sold Miss Silverton this puzzle, so when I received it back in the mail, I was worried there was something wrong with it. Instead, it had a note enclosed asking me to hold it for some friends of hers who would inquire about an owl."

"I can read the characters for you," Wenwen said, "if you put the puzzle together in the right way."

The Detour of the Elephants

"I don't see how this is a puzzle," Benny said. "The pieces don't have pictures on them."

"This is a different kind of puzzle. It's called a tangram and people use it to make shapes," Mr. Yao explained. "Each piece is called a tan. It is very popular here." He motioned to a display shelf.

The Place of Many Puzzles

It was full of puzzles just like the one the Aldens had. "Tangrams first became well known in China during a period in history called the Tang Dynasty. That was more than one thousand years ago. Each tangram can make many, many shapes depending on how you arrange the pieces."

"The easiest one is a rectangle," Wenwen said. She quickly arranged the pieces so they made one big rectangle.

"Can you read the words now?" Henry asked.

Wenwen leaned over. "No, it's just random characters. We should try a different shape, though it will take a very long time to try all the shapes."

"We need to open the envelope to figure out what to do next," Henry said. "I'm sure there is another riddle in it."

CHAPTER 4

Cable Car Caper

"Can I open it?" Violet asked. Henry handed her the envelope. "It's a riddle," she said as she pulled out a piece of paper." She read it out loud.

> *Twelve animals are important, but you need*
> *   only two.*
> *One is very loyal and will never let you down.*
> *The other is not liked by all but is very clever,*
> *   as you must be to complete your tasks.*
> *Each animal will guide you to your next stop.*
> *But beware. Trust those in front of you but*
> *   no others.*

"Twelve? That sounds familiar," Jessie said. "I

know what it means. We learned it last year. The Chinese calendar is separated into twelve-year cycles. Each year has an animal that goes with it. I memorized the animals. Let's see if I can remember." She thought for a moment and then rattled off a list. "Rat, ox, tiger, rabbit, dragon, snake, horse, goat, monkey, rooster, dog, and pig."

"That's correct. Very good," Mr. Yao said.

Violet repeated part of the riddle. *"One is very loyal and will never let you down.* I know that one. It's a dog, just like Watch. He's loyal and never lets us down."

"I believe you are right," Mr. Yao said. "Can you make a dog out of these shapes?"

The Aldens tried several ways to make a dog but couldn't get it just right. "Wenwen, you know how to do this, don't you?" Jessie asked.

"I do," Wenwen said. "I can show you or I can give you a hint."

"A hint, please," Henry said. He was determined to figure it out.

"When you are done, the dog will look like a breed of dog called a Scottish terrier," she said. "Do you know that kind of dog?"

The Detour of the Elephants

"Yes!" Soo Lee said. "They are little black dogs. One of our neighbors had one. They have short ears and short legs and a square face! Maybe the square tan is the dog's face."

With that hint they were able to make a dog shape. The Chinese characters on the pieces made four lines.

"Can you read them, Wenwen?" Benny asked.

"I can read the top and the bottom line. The top says *Doctor*. The bottom line says *Village*. The other characters don't make sense."

"Maybe we need to flip those pieces, since there are characters on the other side too." Jessie flipped over the middle pieces.

"I can read it all now. It says, *Dr. Zhang, Mutianyu Village*."

"Finally!" Henry said. "We are getting closer. Now for the next part." He read off the line about the second animal. *The other is not liked by all but is very clever.*

"Which of those animals don't people like?" Violet asked.

Jessie recited the list again. "Rat, ox, tiger, rabbit,

dragon, snake, horse, goat, monkey, rooster, dog, and pig."

"Some people don't like snakes," Soo Lee said.

"Mrs. McGregor doesn't like rats," Benny said.

Henry flipped all the pieces over. "I think it's a rat. Rats are very clever. They can learn to go through mazes to find food and learn how to use levers to get what they want. I've never heard anyone say a snake was clever."

"Okay, let's try to make a rat shape," Jessie said.

The rat turned out to be hard to make. Wenwen had to show them how. "It takes practice," she said.

"I'm glad you know how to do these," Jessie said. "Can you read it?"

"Yes, it says *Wanli Changcheng*."

"Oh, we thought we might get to go to the Great Wall," Benny said. He was disappointed. "I wanted to stand on top of it."

Mr. Yao smiled. "You will get to go. *Wanli Changcheng* are the Chinese words for the Great Wall. The words have a few different meanings, but I like to tell visitors it means a very long wall."

"Is Mutianyu Village near a part of the Great

Wall?" Henry asked Mr. Yao.

"Yes, it's at the base of a section of the wall that is very popular with tourists. It's not too far from Beijing."

Jessie looked at the clock behind the counter. "It's getting late. Dr. Zhang won't be there at night."

"Let's return the bikes and then go to our hotel," Henry suggested. "We'll go in the morning. I'll call Mary to come get us at the bike rental shop."

"Thank you for helping us, Mr. Yao," Jessie said.

"You're very welcome." He picked up one of the cloth animals. It was yellow and red and black and had a smile on its face. "Miss Silverton also arranged for each of you to have one of these. Please feel free to pick out whichever one you want."

"What are they?" Violet asked. "Are they cats?"

"They are a special kind of cat," he replied. "They are tigers. Tigers mean many things in China. They can be a symbol of strength and bravery. Even though they aren't puzzles, I like them very much so I keep them in my shop."

"I love them!" Violet said.

"Me too!" Soo Lee cried.

Everyone picked out a tiger of their own. They put them in their camera bags and then said good-bye to Mr. Yao.

Wenwen showed them the way back. They dropped of the bikes and then Wenwen said, "I should go home too. I have to go to school tomorrow."

"Thank you very much for helping us," Jessie said. "We couldn't have figured out the riddle without you."

"You're welcome. It was fun." They exchanged email addresses, promising to stay in touch. Wenwen got back on her bike and waved good-bye as she rode away.

Henry called the phone number Mary had given them. It didn't take her long to arrive.

"Did you have a good day?" she asked when they climbed into the van.

"We did," Jessie said. "And we'll need to be driven somewhere else tomorrow, but we'll let you know exactly where and when you pick us up." Jessie had been thinking about the last riddle and the part about trusting no one but who was in front of them. She didn't know if that meant Mary or not. In the morning, Mary would have to know where they were going, but Jessie was uneasy about telling her in advance.

"That's fine," Mary said. "I'll pick you up at whatever time you need to leave. You're going to like your hotel. It used to be a house for an official at the imperial court, and it's built in a traditional style called a courtyard residence. There is a lovely inner courtyard with a pool full of big goldfish called koi."

She turned down a street that was so narrow the van barely fit on it. "These types of streets are called hutongs," she explained. "They are full of old buildings like your hotel. It's a very special area of Beijing."

Violet said, "I'm glad we are getting to see so much. This is a nice city to visit."

When they pulled up in front of the hotel, Jessie arranged for Mary to pick them back up at eight o'clock the next morning.

The hotel was as nice as Mary had described. Benny, Soo Lee, and Violet got to feed the koi while

Henry and Jessie went to find Cousin Joe and Cousin Alice. They all met back in the courtyard.

"Is it time to eat again?" Benny asked. "Solving all those riddles made me very hungry."

"It is," Cousin Alice said. "The clerk at the hotel recommends the restaurant right next door."

The restaurant was much fancier than the dumpling restaurant. A glass roof covered a courtyard full of tables. The courtyard opened at one end to a garden of tall bamboo that had a stone path winding through it.

"It's almost like eating outside!" Violet said as they sat down at a table near the garden.

"A garden inside a restaurant is a great idea," Jessie said. "And I can't wait to try the food."

They ordered something called a tasting menu so they could try several different dishes. Once the food arrived and they were eating the spring rolls and rice balls and fruit dishes, Henry and Jessie explained their plans for the following day.

"We haven't seen any signs of the Argents, so I hope we can deliver the artifact without any problems," Henry said.

"I hope so too," Cousin Joe said. "This has been a very pleasant trip so far."

After dinner they were all very tired. Cousin Alice tried to hide a yawn when she said, "Why don't we all turn in? Traveling tired me out."

***

The next morning after breakfast, Jessie said to the others, "We'd better take our backpacks and everything with us. We don't know if we'll be coming back here. We never know when we are going to get a new clue," she explained to Cousin Alice and Cousin Joe.

Henry called Mary, and they gathered in the lobby to wait for her to arrive.

"How long will it take to get to that village? Mutan...something?" Benny asked.

The hotel clerk overheard Benny. She asked, "Do you mean Mutianyu by the Great Wall?"

Benny nodded.

"It's not far," the woman said. "About one and a half hours."

Jessie wished Benny hadn't asked. Though there was no one else in the lobby besides the clerk, the note had said not to let anyone know where they were going.

Mary arrived and Jessie explained where they wanted to go. "Oh, you'll have fun there!" Mary exclaimed. "I'm glad you are getting to see some sites."

Everyone was quiet on the ride except for Benny and Soo Lee, who played with their cloth tigers and tried to think of names for them.

When Mary pulled into a parking lot and announced they had arrived, Benny said, "I don't see a wall."

Mary laughed, "You'll see it when you get out and look up."

Everyone jumped out of the van. The wall was far above them, way up on top of a steep slope. Benny's mouth dropped open. "It looks a lot bigger than it did on the poster!"

"In many places, the wall was built to run across the tops of mountain ridges," Mary explained. "That made it even more difficult for invaders to cross. I'll be waiting down here when you've seen everything," she said. "I'm going to get some coffee and read a book I brought while I wait. Take as much time as you need."

Everyone got their camera cases and Henry took the duffel bag as well. They walked through the parking lot and into an area where people were selling souvenirs, hats, and arts and crafts.

"There's a sign for Mutianyu Village," Henry said. "I hope it's not very big. I don't know how we are supposed to find Dr. Zhang there."

The village wasn't very large. They walked around looking at some of the older buildings until they saw a sign with both Chinese characters and English words on it. The English part read, Mutianyu Guest House and Restaurant.

"Let's go ask there," Jessie suggested.

Inside they found a woman at a reception desk working on a laptop. She looked up and smiled. "Can I help you? I'm afraid we have no rooms available, but our restaurant is open."

"We are looking for someone," Henry said. "Some-one named Dr. Zhang. Do you know her? Or him? We don't know if Dr. Zhang is a man or a woman."

"Yes, of course," the woman responded. "Dr. Zhang

is a woman. She is staying here while she works on a book, but today she is on top of the wall, showing a group of visiting students around."

"We'd like to see her as soon as possible," Jessie said. "Would we be able to find her if we went to the top of the wall?"

"Yes, unless you pass her coming down as you go up. She'll be with a large group of young people. She is about the age of this lady and gentleman," the woman said smiling at Cousin Joe and Cousin Alice. "Dr. Zhang carries a cane with her, though she doesn't use it all the time. It has a silver dragon head for a handle. You should be able to recognize that."

"What is the best way to get to the top?" Henry asked. "Is there a path?"

"There is, but it's quite a long ways to the top. It's about four thousand steps and will take you more than an hour to hike. If you want to get up more quickly, there is a cable car you can ride."

"Let's take the cable car," Violet said. "That sounds like fun."

"Yes," Jessie said. "I'd like to find Dr. Zhang as soon as we can."

The Detour of the Elephants

The woman from the guesthouse told them how to find the ticket booth for the cable car. They bought tickets and then went to wait in line.

"These look like cable cars at ski resorts," Benny said as he watched the bright orange cars go up the mountain. "I didn't know they used cable cars in other places."

"It's a good way to get up high," Jessie said. "And since they are all enclosed, people can go up and down even in bad weather."

The platform they were waiting on was very crowded. "Stay close," Jessie said to the others. "We don't want to get separated." They inched forward as the people in front of them got on their cars. When it was their turn, the operator asked how many were in their group. Cousin Joe replied, "Seven."

"You'll need two cars then," the man said. He directed Cousin Joe, Cousin Alice, and Soo Lee to one. "The rest of you can go up in the next one." Cousin Joe, Cousin Alice, and Soo Lee got into their car, and Soo Lee waved good-bye through the window.

Cable Car Caper

The next cable car came up the platform, and the man directed the children inside. Jessie, Benny, and Violet were already in when someone on the platform behind Henry yelled, "Watch out!" in a scared voice. Henry stumbled forward into the car, but a person outside the car reached in and took hold of the strap on the duffel bag. Henry tried to grab it back, but the bag was yanked off Henry's shoulder as the door closed. "Wait!" Henry yelled, but the car was already moving away from the station. The duffel bag was gone.

On the Earth Dragon's Back

"Who did that?" Jessie cried as they all crowded around the back of the car trying to see who on the platform had the duffel bag.

"I don't see the bag," Violet said. "There are too many people." Some of them were pointing up at the cable car. Others were turning around like they were trying to see what was happening.

"It was someone who had on a dark blue coat," Benny said. "I saw the coat sleeve."

"I did too," Henry added. "I think it was a woman. I saw a hand on the strap. It was someone with long fingers and painted red fingernails."

"I see someone with a blond ponytail and a blue coat. There," Jessie said. They could see a tall woman walking away from the platform. She had the duffel bag slung over one shoulder.

"Anna Argent," Violet said.

"I can't believe she found us here," Jessie said. Anna Argent had already tried to steal artifacts from them in other places. She was very clever and very quick.

Henry sat down on one of the benches in the car. "We knew the Argents were going to try something like that, but it just surprised me. I didn't expect it to be here."

"It's a good thing it was a decoy bag," Jessie said as she sat down too. "All the artifacts are still safe." She patted her camera bag.

"I wish I knew how they found us," Henry said. "The only people who knew where we were going were Mary, Wenwen, and the owner of the puzzle shop. Tricia said we could trust Wenwen and Mr. Yao."

"Maybe Mary called someone after we went to the village," Violet said.

"They wouldn't have had time to get here," Henry responded. "Unless someone was following the van all the way from Beijing."

Jessie knew there was one other person. She got out her phone and called the hotel. The clerk answered. Jessie explained who she was and then asked, "Did anyone call for us?"

"Yes," the hotel clerk said. "Right after you left. The person said they needed to get in touch with you right away. I was lucky I knew where you were going. I hope they found you."

"Yes, they did," Jessie said. She didn't tell the clerk they didn't want to be found. "Did the caller tell you their name?"

"It was a man by the name of John Smith," the clerk said.

"Thank you." Jessie hung up the phone and then told the others what the clerk said. "Someone made up the name John Smith to find out where we were."

"That's very sneaky!" Violet cried.

"Whoever took it isn't going to be happy when they realize they've been tricked," Henry said.

"Good!" Benny said. "We don't want them to be happy."

"No, we don't, but we want them to go away and not try again," Henry told him.

"Maybe they won't open the packages until they are a long way from here," Violet said.

"I hope they don't," Jessie said as she looked back down the slope. "If they open them right away, they will either follow us to the top of the wall or wait for us when we come down."

That made all of them nervous.

"We should at least be able to get the artifact to Dr. Zhang safely," Henry said.

As they came closer to the wall, it seemed to grow bigger and bigger. "It's so big, it even has little buildings on top!" Benny exclaimed.

"I think those are watchtowers," Henry said. "They kept watch all year long, even in winter."

"I see Soo Lee!" Violet said. "She's waving at us."

When they got off the cable car, they explained to the others what had happened.

"Those Argents are no good," Cousin Joe declared.

"They aren't," Henry said. "But we can find ways to fool them, even Anna."

"I'm glad you thought of the camera bags, Henry," Cousin Alice said.

"I hope that Anna doesn't follow us up here!" Soo Lee said, looking around at the other tourists.

"We'll keep the other artifacts safe," Jessie told her. "Let's find Professor Zhang so we can deliver the one to her."

They walked up the wall where a large group of young people stood listening to a Chinese woman. The woman had a cane with her.

"I'm sure that's Dr. Zhang," Henry said. "And those people listening to her look like students because they are taking notes in notebooks."

They stood at the back of the group until the woman was finished speaking. As the group moved away, the woman saw them. She came over. "Hello," she said. "Can I help you?"

"We have something for you if you are Dr. Zhang," Jessie said.

"I am." She looked around at all of the Aldens, a confused expression on her face. "There are so many of you. I was told to expect one person, a person who liked owls."

The Detour of the Elephants

"We all like owls. It's a long story," Henry said. He took the case inside his camera bag and punched in the code. Opening the lid, he held it out to Dr. Zhang so she could see the clay disk.

Her confused look changed to an excited look. "I am so glad to see that!" she exclaimed.

"We don't know what it is," Violet said.

"It is a chess piece, a very old handmade chess piece. Recently pieces were found in one of the guardhouses, and this is one of them. They are very special," said Dr. Zhang.

"Why?" Benny asked. "I know it's old, but it's just a piece of clay. It looks like it was easy to make."

"I'm sure it was easy to make," Dr. Zhang said. "This find was so interesting because we don't have many written records about the lives of ordinary soldiers who were stationed here. Often, history is written about the leaders and the generals but not about the people who did much of the work."

"Some other archaeologists we have met told us that too," Jessie said.

"Yes, we are lucky that in China we have written records of much of our history. Many places don't have that, though of course they had their own civilizations."

"It doesn't look like a chess piece to me," Violet said.

"Did you know there is more than one kind of chess?" Dr. Zhang asked.

"No," Henry said. "I thought all chess was the same."

"People in China play what you think of as chess, which is sometimes called the international version," Dr. Zhang said. "But they also play a version called Xiangqi. It's one of the most popular board games in China. This is a Xiangqi piece. The game represents a battle between two armies, with the object of capturing the enemy's general. The pieces are flat disks like this, with characters on them. Of course now they aren't made of clay, but this is clearly a Xiangqi piece. It was probably made by one of the soldiers who wanted to play the game."

"I thought the soldiers were supposed to be watching out for invaders," Violet said. "How could they have time to play chess?"

"There were many, many soldiers here and they worked in shifts. They lived here, in structures built along the bottom of the wall, so when they were off duty they had some free time, though they also had other jobs. Some of their time was even spent farming. It took a large amount of food to feed the up to one million soldiers who were stationed along the wall. This area is known for its fruit trees, so the soldiers tended to the orchards."

"I didn't know soldiers did jobs like that," Henry said.

"Yes, soldiers then had to do all sorts of jobs." Dr. Zhang continued. "You're seeing a part of the wall that was built more recently. Some parts of the wall are much older. They may have been built two thousand five hundred years ago, or even more. Then they were rebuilt through the years. Today some parts are still in very good condition. At other places along the wall, sections have disappeared or are in poor repair."

"Can we go in one of the watchtowers?" Benny asked.

"Of course," Dr. Zhang said. "Come this way."

She led them inside one. "There would have been some sort of cooking pot in here and stools as well back when it was in use."

"It's not as cozy as our boxcar," Violet said. It was dark and damp inside the watchtower. She tried to imagine what it had been like when it was full of soldiers. She could see why they would have wanted to play games when they were done working.

"It isn't very cozy, is it?" Dr. Zhang asked. "Some of these buildings were used for more than just staying out of the weather. Soldiers used part of them to communicate long distances. There were no telephones of course, so they had to think of a different way to let other soldiers know if invaders were coming. Can you guess how they did it?"

"No," Benny replied. "I guess they could send letters, or send people to take messages."

"That's good thinking," Dr. Zhang said. "They could do that, but sometimes they needed a way to get a message somewhere fast. At those times, they lit signal fires up on the flat roofs. There were ways to make fires very smoky, so that's what they did during the day. If they needed to signal at night, they lit regular fires. That's why these watch towers are flat on top and made of stone. They could light beacon fires on the top of them. If you'd like to see more, I can walk with you for a while, but then I need to get back to work."

They explored the top of the wall with her, and then it was time to get back down. "Do we ride the cable car back down or do we walk?" Violet asked.

"There's another way you might like," Dr. Zhang said. "Follow me." She led them farther along the wall. When she stopped, they could see people in a line at the bottom of the wall.

"What are they waiting for?" Benny asked.

"An exciting way down," Dr. Zhang said. "It's called a toboggan ride, but there is a metal chute for the sleds instead of riding on snow."

"That looks like fun!" Jessie said. "Should we try it?" she asked the others.

They all decided they wanted to go, so they took the staircase down the wall to the line for the sleds.

The operator of the ride explained how the sleds worked. They had brakes by the riders' feet. He told the Aldens that the younger children could ride with the older ones, so Benny shared a sled with Jessie. Soo Lee rode down with Violet and Henry came next. Cousin Joe and Cousin Alice had their own sleds and came down last.

The chute wound down the mountain. It was like going on an amusement park ride in a forest. The Aldens sped down the hill, putting on the brakes when signs along the way told them to slow down.

"Whee!" Violet and Soo Lee cried out together.

"Hurry, Jessie!" Benny called out. "They'll catch us!"

"They may catch us, but they can't pass us!" Jessie told him. The chute was only wide enough for one sled at a time. They could hear Henry, Cousin Joe, and Cousin Alice laughing behind them.

The ride came to an end in a long flat section, so the sleds could slow down and finally come to a stop.

"That was so much fun!" Soo Lee said as she and Violet got off.

"It was," Jessie agreed. She was relieved they had delivered another artifact safely.

Once everyone was off, they walked back

through the village, stopped to get a snack, and then walked to the parking lot. As they got closer to the van, they could see Mary waving excitedly at them.

She hurried toward them. "I was hoping you'd come down soon. I have an important message. Your pilot called. You need to get to the airport right away to catch a flight to Bangkok, Thailand. It leaves in three hours. We'll just have time to get you there and checked in."

The Man in the Green Van

It took a minute for everyone to understand what Mary was trying to tell them. Jessie asked her to repeat what she had said.

After she was done, Henry asked. "Do you mean we are taking a commercial flight? Not the Reddimus Society plane?"

"Yes, a commercial flight," Mary replied. "The pilot said there's a mechanical problem with the plane, and there is no time to wait for repairs. Let's go. I don't want you to miss your plane. I'll tell you the rest of the message once we are on our way."

They all hurried to the van, and Mary pulled out onto the road. There was more traffic than there had been earlier in the day. "I hope we get there in time," she said.

"What was the rest of the message?" Jessie asked.

"Once you land in Thailand, you are to go to the Elephant Wildlife Reserve. Then you'll get your clue as to where you go next."

"Elephants!" Soo Lee cried. "Yay! I love elephants."

"I do too," Violet said. "This will be fun."

"I hope so. I hope the Reddimus plane can be fixed soon," Henry said. "Thailand is a long way to go to get a clue where to go next."

Because of the heavy traffic, they made it to the airport just in time. At the ticket counter they were surprised there weren't any tickets waiting for them.

The airline agent said, "I have your reservations. You just need to pay for the tickets."

"That's strange," Henry said. "Trudy usually arranges all that. I can call her."

"I'll pay for the tickets," Cousin Alice said. "We'll miss the flight if we don't hurry."

The Aldens went through the security line and

then ran to their gate. The other passengers were already boarding. Once everyone was seated on the plane, Benny asked, "Would someone tell me where Thailand is?"

Jessie laughed. "Of course, Benny. I'll show you." She pulled out a magazine from the pocket of the seat in front of them and opened it to a page showing a map of the world. She pointed to a spot on the map. "It's a country that is also in Asia. It's south of China—right here. We are landing at the capital city, Bangkok, which is right here."

"Thailand isn't as big as China," Benny said as he studied the map.

"No, and most of it is very tropical, so it will be warm there," Henry said.

The flight took about five hours. When the plane landed, they got off and Jessie said, "I suppose someone will be here to meet us. The Silvertons have been arranging that for us everywhere we go."

They stood for a time outside the gate but no one approached them. Finally, Henry went up to an information booth and talked to the woman there. He came back to report what he had learned.

"There aren't any messages for us here," he said. "The woman at the desk suggested we go out to where the drivers wait to pick up passengers. The driver might be there."

"I'm sure we'll find someone out there," Cousin Alice said.

Cousin Joe exchanged some US money for Thai money, and then they walked through the airport.

"It's the most beautiful airport I've ever seen," Violet said. Huge colorful statues representing parts of Thai culture were placed around the central areas of the terminals. Many of them were painted gold. The curved glass ceiling let in light from the sun, which was setting, and the light made the statues look like they were glowing.

"I read on the plane that the name of the airport means The Golden Land." Henry said. "The article had lots of pictures of all the golden temples and statues in Thailand."

They continued through the airport, admiring all the statues until they came to the spot where drivers waited.

"There's someone with an Alden sign," Violet

said. She motioned to the group of drivers. One man stood out. He was a very big man with messy red hair, a beard, and wire-rimmed glasses. "He doesn't look much like the other drivers," she said doubtfully.

"He doesn't, does he?" Cousin Alice said. "He looks like a tourist who lost his suitcase and has only one outfit to wear."

The man had on baggy shorts and a grubby shirt that had a button missing. He was wearing sandals. One of the sandals had a broken strap.

"Maybe our trip was so rushed, he was the only one available," Jessie suggested, though she felt uneasy about the man.

Henry walked up to him. "Hello, we're the Aldens."

The man took a step back, nearly dropping the sign. "Oh yes," he stuttered. "Good. You're here." The man spoke with an English accent like some of the people they had heard when they had delivered one of the artifacts to Stonehenge.

"Hurry, my car is in the parking lot," the man said. He looked around at them. "Do you have all your things?" he asked. He was staring down at Benny's camera bag.

"Yes we do," Henry said

"Follow me then," the man said as he turned to leave. "The Silvertons want you on your way as soon as possible."

He led them to a very old, rusty green van. When he opened the door, they could see it was full of food wrappers and empty drink cans.

He said, "Sorry for the mess," as he brushed some of the trash off the passenger seat.

"How far is it?" Jessie asked.

"Not far," the man said. His phone rang. He answered and said, "Yes, I have them," and then he hung up.

Jessie's feeling that something was wrong grew stronger. Even though the man had mentioned the Silvertons, he hadn't introduced himself.

She looked over at Henry. He looked back and gave a small shake of his head.

"What do you think of owls?" Jessie asked the man.

"Owls? What are you talking about?" He stared at her, frowning.

"What do you think of owls?" Jessie repeated.

The man scowled. "I don't think about owls. Everybody in. We need to get going. Hurry up."

"Wait, I lost my passport," Henry said, putting his hands on his pockets. "It's not here. It must be back at passport control."

"We'll have to go back and get it," Cousin Joe said. "You've got to have your passport."

"Yes, we need to hurry. I hope you didn't drop it somewhere," Jessie said. "Wait here," she told the red-haired man. "We'll be back." She grabbed Benny's hand. "Come on everyone!"

"Wait! No!" the man yelled as the Aldens darted back into the terminal. "You're supposed to come with me! Come back!"

"Just wait there!" Henry yelled. "We'll be back!"

As soon as they were back in the terminal, Henry led them into a big crowd and then around behind one of the large statues.

"Why did you stop?" Cousin Joe asked. "We need to find your passport."

Henry pulled his passport out of his pocket. "I've had it all along," he said. "I don't trust that man.

I don't think he really works for the Reddimus Society."

"He didn't say anything about owls, and he just didn't look right," Jessie said.

"That's true," Cousin Alice said. "He was a very scruffy man."

"We should call Trudy," Violet said.

"We don't have time," Benny said. "There he is again!"

The man was pushing his way through the crowd looking from side to side.

"He doesn't see us. Let's go get a taxi and get out of here!" Jessie said.

They ran back out of the airport to the line of taxis and found a van that was big enough for all of them.

"Where to?" the taxi driver asked as they jumped inside.

"Uh oh," Violet said. "The man has seen us. He's running toward his car."

"We'd like to go into the city," Jessie said, "and then we'll tell you exactly where to let us off." She turned to the others, "I'm sure there will be so many cars, he won't be able to follow us."

There was a lot of traffic, but every time they looked back, they could still see the green van. Soon they were in the middle of the city.

"He's still following us and he's getting closer!" Violet said, looking out the back window.

The taxi came to a stop. It couldn't move because so many trucks, cars, and motorcycles filled the roads. They were stuck in a giant traffic jam. Jessie noticed the only vehicles moving were the motorcycles and some small three-wheeled vehicles with taxi signs on top of them. They didn't have windows except for a front windshield. Most were full of tourists laughing and taking pictures.

"What are those?" Jessie asked, pointing at one.

"They are called tuk-tuks," the taxi driver explained. "They are very popular with tourists. They don't go very fast, but they will fit down some of our smaller streets and alleys, and they can go around traffic jams."

Henry looked back. "At least the man in the van can't move either," he said.

The Detour of the Elephants

"We'll get out here," Jessie said to the taxi driver. "Thank you. I have an idea," she said to the others as she opened the door. Everyone climbed out as Cousin Joe pulled out some money and paid the driver. They all followed Jessie over to a line of tuk-tuks that were parked waiting for customers.

Jessie went up to one driver who stood by a bright red tuk-tuk. "Could you take us on a tour of Bangkok down some of the small streets where cars can't go?"

"Of course," said the man. "You all won't fit in one though." He called to the man next to him and said something in a different language. The man nodded his head and pointed at his own tuk-tuk, which was yellow.

"I'll take four, and the other three can ride in my friend's vehicle," the red tuk-tuk's driver said.

They climbed into the tuk-tuks. The passenger area had benches on each side to sit on, so Jessie and Benny sat on one side facing Henry and Violet. Cousin Joe, Cousin Alice, and Soo Lee got in the other tuk-tuk.

The traffic on the road was moving again, and

as the tuk-tuks started up, the Aldens could see the green van inching closer.

The tuk-tuks took off down a small side street lined with shops. The red-haired man tried to follow but his van wouldn't fit. People waved him away from the street. He had to back up. The Aldens saw him pounding his hand on the steering wheel, a frustrated look on his face.

"Good riddance to him," Cousin Joe muttered.

CHAPTER

7

A New Suspicion

The tuk-tuk drivers took the Aldens on a winding route through small, busy streets. They saw shops full of flowers, and others of clothing and jewelry. There were many food stands. At one spot the drivers stopped and bought mango juice for everyone. Even though it had gotten dark, the weather was still hot and the cool drinks tasted good.

No one saw the green van anywhere.

"Let's get out of here and try to call Trudy," Henry suggested. "I'm sure the man in the green van doesn't know where we went."

They got out. Henry tried to call Trudy. "Trudy isn't answering," he said. "It might be because of the time change." He left a message for Trudy to call them as soon as possible.

"What do we do now?" Violet asked.

"It's getting late," Cousin Alice said. "I think we should find a hotel."

Jessie agreed. "We can go to the elephant reserve in the morning. We can find out what's happening once we get there."

"Can we take a tuk-tuk there?" Benny asked. "I liked them."

"I looked up information about the elephant reserve," Henry said. "It's miles outside the city. Without a car and a driver, we could take a taxi or a train. I'm sorry, Benny. Tuk-tuks don't go fast enough."

"Trains are good too!" Benny said. "I vote for a train instead of a taxi." They all decided a train would be fun. Cousin Joe found a hotel close by. After a quick dinner in the hotel restaurant, everyone agreed they would go straight to bed so they could get an early start in the morning right after breakfast.

The next morning, Benny woke up early and

made sure everyone else got up too. He was very excited to see the elephants.

A taxi got them to the train station on time. Once they were seated, Benny said, "Now we can forget about that man who chased us."

"I hope so," Jessie said. She didn't point out that the man might realize they had gone on to the elephant reserve. She knew he might try to find them there.

The train passed through some smaller towns and went by farms. "It's all so green and pretty," Violet said as she looked out the window.

The time went by fast. When the train pulled into their station, Benny cried, "There are tuk-tuks here too!" A row of tuk-tuks were lined up next to some regular taxis.

"We can't pass up a chance to ride in tuk-tuks again," Jessie said, smiling at Benny. They piled in and were soon on their way. The reserve wasn't far from the train station.

"I see a sign with an elephant on it!" Violet said. And soon they could see some of the reserve's buildings ahead. They could also see part of a big fenced-in grassy area, where several elephants stood together by a clump of trees.

"I see them!" Benny cried.

After they parked and paid for their ride, a young man wearing a khaki uniform with an elephant logo on his shirt came out of the nearest building.

He came over to them and said, "Welcome to the reserve. The next tour is in ten minutes. I'll be your guide today. My name is Chakrit Banthao."

"We're not here for a tour," Henry said.

"I'm sorry, I misunderstood. Are you here to stay in one of our lodges?" Chakrit waved at some buildings they hadn't noticed. There were large cabins built up on posts right next to a fence enclosing a large grassy area.

"No, not that either," Henry said. "We'd like to take a tour if we had time, but we're here because someone might be expecting us. We're the Aldens."

The young man raised his eyebrows in surprise. "I hadn't heard of any special visitors coming today, but I will check in the office to see who is expecting you. Please wait here."

Before he could walk away, Jessie said, "Maybe

someone is waiting for us who doesn't know our names but knows that we like owls."

"Oh, so you are naturalists?" the man asked. "You study owls?" he asked Cousin Alice.

"No, we don't study them officially or anything, though we certainly like owls," Cousin Alice said. She looked over at Jessie.

"That's right," Jessie said. "We like owls."

"I see," Chakrit said, though his face wore a confused expression. "I'll check in the office," he said again.

He came back a few minutes later. "I'm sorry. No one is expecting anyone named Alden or anyone who works with owls. But you are more than welcome to tour the reserve."

"What do we do now?" Violet asked.

"Thank you," Henry said to Chakrit. "We need a few minutes to figure out what we're doing."

"That's fine. If you'd like to take a tour, meet over at the sign for the elephant kitchen, where we prepare food for the elephants that need special diets." Chakrit went over to a delivery truck that had just pulled into the parking lot.

A New Suspicion

"If no one here is expecting us, does that mean we weren't supposed to come to Thailand at all?" Violet said.

"No, we weren't. Somehow the Argents tricked us," Henry said.

"How do they know so much about what we are doing?" Jessie asked. "Someone called Mary. How did they know who she was and how to call her?"

Henry was quiet for a few moments and then he said, "I think either Emilio or Mr. Ganert is working for the Argents."

Violet let out a gasp.

"It can't be Emilio!" Benny cried. "He's too nice. And he tells good jokes."

"I hope it is not Emilio," Henry said. "But he could be very good at pretending to be nice."

"I think Henry is right," Jessie said. "Emilio and Mr. Ganert have always known where we would be when the Argents found us. They are the only ones besides Trudy, and we know Trudy wouldn't be working with the Argents. I think Tricia suspects one of them. That's why she is leaving us all these riddles and messages to not tell anyone. When we solve the riddles, only members of the Reddimus Society should know where we are going. If the Argents know too, that means either Emilio or Mr. Ganert is giving them information."

"But which one is it?" Violet asked.

"We'll have to figure that out," Henry said.

"And we'll have to do it while we keep the rest of the artifacts safe," Jessie said.

"It's getting late," Cousin Alice said. "We need to figure out what to do for tonight."

"If they have room in the lodge, I think we should stay here," Cousin Joe added.

"So we'll get to see the elephants after all?" Benny asked.

"Yes, let's do that," Jessie said. "That's a good plan."

They went to find Chakrit and asked him about space in the lodge. He made a telephone call and reported there was a cabin available. "Since it is getting late in the day, I can take you on a tour first," he offered. "After that you can check in."

Everyone was eager to see the elephants, so they followed him to a gate that led into a smaller fenced area. Chakrit said, "There are thousands of elephants in Thailand. Some live in the wild and some are in captivity. Elephants used to work in the logging industry. They moved heavy logs that were cut down in areas where there weren't many roads. Now we are trying to preserve our forests and not cut down so many trees. That means there are so many elephants that do not need to work. They can't be released back into the wild though. They can't take care of themselves after living in captivity, so now many of them are in elephant reserves like this. We also rescue elephants that were used in small traveling circuses or for tourist rides in places where they were mistreated."

"Do you have any baby elephants here?" Violet asked.

"We do. We have three calves right now. That's what baby elephants are called."

"Just like baby cows," Benny said. "Except these babies are bigger, aren't they?"

"Yes, elephant calves are much bigger. They weigh about two hundred pounds when they are born. That's as much as some adult humans."

The Detour of the Elephants

Chakrit looked into the fenced-in area. "One of our calves should be right over here." He called, "Saree!"

A little elephant came trotting out from behind some of the bushes.

"It's playing with a soccer ball!" Violet said. The elephant pushed the soccer ball toward them with its trunk. As the calf came closer to them,

two adult elephants followed at a distance. The young elephant seemed very happy, trotting and swinging its trunk. It came up to the gate of the smaller enclosure, which opened into the bigger area. Chakrit opened the gate and the elephant came through pushing the soccer ball. Walking right up to Chakrit, it raised its trunk up so it was resting on his shoulder.

One of the older elephants made a very loud bellowing sound. Benny and Soo Lee jumped at the noise. "What was that?" Soo Lee asked.

"That's called trumpeting," Chakrit explained. "It's okay, Navann," he called out to the big elephant who was watching them. "Elephants trumpet when they are warning of danger or they are excited. She is warning little Saree here not to go too far away from her," he said, petting the smaller animal. "Saree loves her soccer ball, but she loves people too."

"Saree is a pretty name," Jessie said.

"She is named Saree because it means freedom," Chakrit explained. "She is happy now, but she was very sad when she was rescued because she had been taken away from her mother when she was still too young and made to work in a circus. Some of the older elephants in the reserve help care for her. They are like her grandmothers, aunts, and nannies. In the wild, elephants live in groups and the older elephants take care of the younger ones. It's somewhat like big extended human families."

"That's nice," Violet said. "Just like us. We have a lot of people taking care of us."

"You can pet her if you want," Chakrit said. "She likes attention."

The sound of some voices came from the elephant kitchen. A woman came out the door. "Chakrit, I need some advice," she said.

"If you don't mind waiting here with Saree, I won't be long," Chakrit told the Aldens.

"We don't mind at all," Jessie said. "Getting to pet elephants is terrific."

As soon as Chakrit went inside the building, Jessie's phone rang. It was Trudy. Jessie put the phone on speaker so everyone could hear.

"Trudy, we aren't sure what is going on," Jessie said. "There is no one here to meet us."

The connection wasn't very good. They could

barely hear Trudy. "Where are you?" Trudy cried. "We've been worried sick."

"We're in Thailand," Henry told her. "We got a message we were supposed to get on a flight to Bangkok. And once we arrived, we thought we had to go to an elephant reserve, but we are here at the reserve, and they don't know anything about us. We think we've been tricked."

"It sounds as if you have. We all have been tricked. Is everyone all right?"

"We're fine." Jessie told her about the red-haired man at the airport and how they'd gotten away from him. "I don't think he intended to take us to the reserve at all."

"Say that again. I didn't hear all of that," Trudy said. Jessie repeated herself.

"He probably didn't," Trudy said. "I think he was just going to take you somewhere and demand you hand over the artifacts, then leave you in Thailand while he got away."

"The driver in China told us the message said we didn't have to call Emilio. Was the plane really broken?" Henry asked.

The Detour of the Elephants

There was silence on the other end. "We lost the connection," Jessie said. "I'll try to call her back." Before Jessie could dial, the phone rang again.

"This is a terrible connection," Trudy said. "I may lose you again. Henry, the plane is in perfect shape. As soon as we get off the phone, I'll call Mr. Ganert and tell him they need to come get you. We can't find your driver in Beijing. That's why we had no idea where you'd gone. Her husband told us she'd been hired to drive someone to another city in China. We tried to call her, but she didn't answer her cell phone."

"I hope she's all right," Jessie said. "She was very nice. I'm sure she didn't know we'd been tricked either."

"We'll find her. Are your cousins still with you?"

"Yes, we're all together," Cousin Alice said.

"That's good. I'll make arrangements for somewhere for you to stay tonight until the Reddimus plane can get to you."

"We think we'll stay at the elephant reserve," Jessie said. "They have rooms here and the people who run the place are very nice."

A New Suspicion

"That's fine, if that's where you'd like to stay."

"We would." Henry was just about to tell her their suspicions about Emilio and Mr. Ganert when they got cut off again. Jessie tried to call her back but there was no answer.

"We'll tell her when we get back to Bangkok," Jessie said. "Maybe we can figure out a way to know which one is working for the Argents before then."

"I hope so." Violet gave a shudder. "We have to get back on the plane with them. I don't want to be flown around by someone working for the Argents."

The Detour of the Elephants

They petted the little elephant while they talked about ideas, but no one could come up with a good plan.

Chakrit came back just as one of the adult elephants walked over to a branch that lay on the ground. The elephant picked it up with her trunk and then used it to shoo some flies away that were swarming around her shoulder.

"That's funny!" Soo Lee said. "She made her own flyswatter."

"Elephants are very intelligent," Chakrit said. "Even young elephants can be very clever. I heard a story about a group of young elephants who had to wear bells around their necks so their keepers knew if they wandered off. Some of the young elephants learned how to stuff mud into the bells each night so they could sneak away and eat bananas at a neighboring farm. Elephants love bananas."

"That was very smart," Henry said.

"It was. The keepers could hear the other elephants moving around their own area, but since there wasn't any sound of elephants moving out of the area, they didn't suspect anything was amiss. The next morning the farmer came over to complain, and that's when they noticed the young elephants' bells weren't making any noise."

Chakrit pointed at a wooden box up in one of the trees. It had two ropes attached to it. "There aren't many animal species that will figure out how to work together to complete a task. Chimps and dolphins are some that do, and we've now learned that elephants do as well. A researcher designed an experiment where elephants could get at a treat in a box only if two worked together to pull on a rope. We've tried it here, and our elephants figured it out very quickly. I'm sure in the wild they work together in other ways we haven't learned yet." He patted the little elephant again and said, "Enough attention for you." Chakrit led Saree back into the main area. She pushed her ball over to the bigger elephants, and then three of them moved away.

When Chakrit returned to where the Aldens stood, he smiled and said, "Many of our visitors like to help out with some chores around the reserve. Are you interested?"

Everyone was very excited to help. They spent the rest of the day preparing food and then taking it to the elephants. Chakrit took them to watch some elephants bathing in a river and then they helped plant some small shrubs along one of the fences.

Late in the afternoon, Chakrit looked at his watch. "We are about to close up this part of the reserve for the night, but you will be able to see elephants from your rooms. There are big decks on all of them that are right outside the fence. That's why we've raised up the cabins on posts."

The Aldens followed Chakrit to the lodge's lobby to check in, and then outside to go to their cabin. As they went, Soo Lee, Benny, and Violet talked excitedly about Saree and the other elephants. But Henry was distracted by something across the road from the reserve's entrance. There, in the parking lot of an old gas station, was the red-haired man. Henry watched him get into the rusty van, where he pulled out a drink and a bag of chips and settled back in the seat. Henry took Jessie's arm and pointed across the road.

When she saw the man her face fell. "He came here after all," she whispered. "I think he's waiting for us to leave, and then he's going to follow us."

"Yes," Henry said. "I don't like this."

After a little while, they arrived at their cabin and couldn't talk more. "This is amazing!" Benny cried as Chakrit opened the door for them. Benny and Soo Lee ran around into each of the rooms exploring. There were three bedrooms that opened onto a central living room. All the rooms had lots of windows. From the living room, they could walk out through sliding glass doors to a big deck. Elephants were only a few feet away from them on the other side of the fence.

Chakrit said, "Call the main lodge or come back

to the front desk if you need anything. I'll be here a few more hours doing some paperwork, but anyone else here will help you too."

Everyone went out on the deck to watch the elephants. "I have an idea about Mr. Ganert and Emilio," Jessie said. "But it's complicated, and it depends on our cell phones working."

"Let's hear it," Henry said.

She explained how they had seen the red-haired man across the road. No one was happy with that news.

"We should call the police and have him arrested," Cousin Alice declared.

"He hasn't done anything yet," Cousin Joe pointed out. "No one would arrest him for offering to give us a ride. We can't prove he intended to steal the artifacts."

"We can't prove that, but we can see if he does try to steal something," Jessie said. "My plan is that we pretend we are going back to Bangkok. He'll follow us, but somehow along the way we will turn around or get another taxi back here. Then we'll call Emilio and Mr. Ganert and tell them we are here. If the man comes back here to find us, we'll know one of them called him."

Henry thought for a moment. "That's a good plan," he said. "We are going to need some help though. We can ask Chakrit. I think we can trust him. He can help us figure out how to switch taxis and get back here."

They went to find Chakrit. Jessie said, "We need some help."

"Of course," Chakrit said. "What can I do?"

"This will sound strange, but there is a man trying to steal something from us. He followed us here from Bangkok, and he's in a van across the road. We'd like him to think we are going back into Bangkok instead of spending the night here. We'd like to have a taxi take us partway back to Bangkok, but let us off somewhere halfway. Then we can come back here and spend the night. We'll pay for the taxi to keep going into the city so if someone is following it, they won't know where we've gone. That means the taxi will have to pull over someplace where we can jump out and hide until we can arrange for another taxi to pick us up.

The Detour of the Elephants

Can you think of how we can do that?"

Chakrit was very surprised by Jessie's story. "That is a very bad trick to play on visitors to our country," he said. "Do you know who it is? I can contact the police and report it."

"We don't know the person's name, but he isn't from Thailand." Henry described the man and his English accent. "We aren't sure the police could do anything because the man hasn't tried to steal anything yet. We just want him to go away. That's why Jessie came up with the plan for the taxis."

"I'll certainly help you," Chakrit said. "I know how you can do this. My friends own a restaurant on the way back to Bangkok. To reach it, a car goes up a big hill, and right after the hill it turns into the driveway. There are many plants in front of the restaurant. A taxi can pull in and let you out and then continue on its way. Then the owners of the restaurant will call you a taxi back here."

"That is a good idea," Jessie said. "Thank you."

"Let me make some telephone calls."

"Alice and Soo Lee and I will stay here," Cousin Joe said. "We won't all fit in a taxi anyway, and the red-haired man knows it's you four who are carrying the artifacts." He patted his stomach. "I am getting hungry though. Should we meet you at the restaurant a little later so we can all eat dinner?"

"Yes," Benny said, patting his own stomach. "I'm hungry too."

Henry invited Chakrit to come eat with them and the man agreed. It took only a few minutes for the taxi to arrive. Violet was nervous about the plan but tried to act as if she wasn't. The taxi driver was very nice, though he was surprised at what Chakrit asked him to do. Cousin Joe paid him in advance so the children could jump out and hide as fast as possible.

Once they were inside the taxi, Jessie leaned out the window, waved, and called to Chakrit, "Thank you for showing us around. We'll bring our Grandfather back some day." She wasn't sure the red-haired man could hear them from across the road, but she thought it was worth a try.

Chakrit played along and waved back. "Good-bye. Enjoy the rest of your visit!"

They didn't see any other cars on the road for

quite a while. Henry said, "I hope he saw us leave."

"Me too," Benny said. "I don't want to go back to the lodge if he's still watching for us."

Violet had been watching out the back window. When the road straightened out, she gave a start and then sank down in the seat. "I see the green van," she whispered in a scared voice.

"I don't see anything," Jessie said, looking out the back window. "No, wait, yes I do. I see the van. He was watching for us."

The van drew closer to the taxi. "I'm not sure our plan is going to work," Henry said.

"Keep your fingers crossed," Jessie said. "How close are we?" she asked the taxi driver.

"We are very close. It's just over the next hill," the man said.

"Is everybody ready?" Jessie asked. The others nodded. The taxi sped up and came up over the hill. They could see a driveway to the right and a sign that read The Orchid Restaurant.

The driver pulled in. "Everybody out and hide!" Henry said. He and Violet scrambled out. Jessie started to get out but Benny cried. "I can't

get my seat belt off!" She turned back and helped him unbuckle it. They both jumped out of the car and ran together to hide behind a big clump of plants covered in flowers. Henry and Violet were already behind some plants that looked like short palm trees.

The taxi pulled back out on the road and headed in the direction of Bangkok. The Aldens waited. "I hope the red-haired man doesn't turn in here," Henry said. "If he does, everyone run inside the restaurant. We'll ask for help in there."

"I see the van," Violet said. They all looked back to the road. The van was just coming up over the hill. Everyone held very still.

Benny whispered, "Go right on by. Go right on by."

CHAPTER 9

Caught in the Act

The van slowed. Jessie said, "Get ready to run inside." Just as they thought the van was going to turn into the restaurant drive, it sped up and drove right by, continuing down the road. The red-haired man didn't even look in their direction.

Jessie let out a sigh of relief.

"Yay!" Benny said. "The trick worked!"

Everyone came out from their hiding places, happy the first part of the plan worked. Jessie got out her cell phone and dialed Emilio. He answered, sounding very happy to hear from them. "We were worried!" he said. "We'll be there tomorrow to get you. We are taking off early in the morning. Is everyone okay?"

The Detour of the Elephants

"We're fine," Jessie said. "We are staying at a terrific place." She told him all about the lodge and the elephants.

"That sounds like fun," Emilio said.

"Is Mr. Ganert with you?" Henry asked.

"He is. He's been listening in," Emilio said.

"Good," Jessie said. "We'll see you tomorrow." She hung up the phone. "Now they both know. We'll see what happens next."

A taxi pulled up with Cousin Joe, Cousin Alice, Soo Lee, and Chakrit. They were happy to hear the red-haired man hadn't even noticed the Aldens had gotten out of the taxi. Everyone went inside the restaurant, ready to enjoy themselves. Chakrit ordered for all of them.

"This is the best food ever!" Benny declared.

"I thought you said the dumplings in Beijing were the best ever," Cousin Alice teased.

"They were. Lots of food can be the best ever!"

Once everyone was finished, Henry said, "I've been thinking. As soon as it is dark, it will be hard to tell if the red-haired man has come back. We need to know for sure. Let's go back and I'll explain my plan on the way."

As they rode back in the taxi, Henry told them the details. "We need to use one of the empty camera bags as a decoy. We can set it out on the deck. If the red-haired man comes back and really wants to steal something, he'll come sneaking around to see if he can break in. He won't be able to resist taking a camera bag."

"I don't like the idea of someone sneaking around the reserve," Chakrit said. "It will disturb the elephants."

"I don't like the idea either," Benny said.

"I'll leave my camera bag out on the deck," Violet said. She took the wooden box holding the artifact case out of the bag.

"I suppose we should put the wooden box in the camera case," Jessie said. "If someone takes the case, they'll check to see if there is anything inside it. They'll know the empty cardboard box in there doesn't weigh enough to hold an artifact."

"We could put some little stones inside the wooden box," Violet said.

"Yes, that's a good idea," Henry said. "I wish we

had some way to make it more difficult for them. The wooden box is too easy to open."

"We have some padlocks," Chakrit said. "You could lock it up with one of those."

"If they steal the case, the padlock will be stolen too," Jessie pointed out.

"That's all right. If it will fool thieves, I don't mind. I can easily get another."

Back at the reserve, Chakrit went to get the padlock and then joined them in the living room of the cabin.

"If he's coming back, he should be here soon," Cousin Joe said. "We were at the restaurant long enough for him to go to Bangkok and back. Or he might be here already if he caught up to the taxi and saw you weren't in it any longer."

Henry and Jessie had been talking. Jessie said, "Henry and I are going to go hide outside and watch for him. If he tries to steal the case, we'll yell at him, and then he'll know we know who it is. That may make him go away."

"I will go over to the store to see if his van is there," Chakrit said. "If he gets away with the case,

I will have his license plate number and we can report him."

They fixed up the camera case with the padlocked wooden box and set it on the deck. Chakrit left to go see if he could find the van.

"We want the man to think we aren't paying any attention," Henry said. "We need to be like the elephants Chakrit told us about. Everyone in here, make a lot of noise and pretend we are here too. That way when we hide outside, the man won't know we are waiting for him." They opened all the windows so their voices would carry outside. Chakrit had showed them a cabinet full of games, and Benny picked out a few they could play.

As Henry and Jessie crept down the stairs to find a place to watch, the others talked loudly about which game they wanted to play. "Here's a good spot," Henry said. There was a clump of bushes near the deck growing on both sides of the fence.

They took up spots where they could see most of the deck. It was very dark but the light spilling out from inside lit up the space where the camera bag sat. Jessie and Henry could hear the others inside laughing and talking.

They waited, trying to hold still. Nothing moved, and it was very quiet. Jessie began to wonder if they had been wrong about one of the pilots working for the Argents. Maybe the Argents had figured out another way to follow them everywhere.

All of the sudden, Henry let out a muffled cry and leaped out of the bushes. He scared Jessie, who bolted out of their hiding place too. "What is it?" she whispered.

"Someone touched me on the shoulder," Henry said.

They heard rustling in the bushes. "Who's there?" Jessie said. There wasn't any answer, just more rustling.

"I see someone, or something," Henry said. They both froze.

The shape came closer. Jessie burst out giggling.

"Jessie, why are you laughing?" Henry asked.

She giggled again. "It's Saree." The little elephant came up to them and reached through the fence with her trunk.

Henry let out a sigh of relief. "Saree, we don't

really need your help." They petted her, not knowing what else to do.

Henry froze again. "I see someone moving over there," he whispered and pointed into the elephant area.

The Detour of the Elephants

As Jessie watched, she could make out a figure creeping closer and closer to the deck. It was so dark, she couldn't see very clearly, but she was almost sure it was the red-haired man. Just as the figure reached up to climb up on the deck, an elephant trumpeted close by. Jessie and Henry were both so startled, they let out shrieks of surprise. The elephant trumpeted again. An adult elephant lumbered toward Saree. The little elephant trotted up to the larger elephant and then followed it away.

"Look," Henry said. "The camera case is gone."

CHAPTER

10

Back on Track

Henry and Jessie went back inside and explained what had happened. "Now we know either Emilio or Mr. Ganert can't be trusted," Henry said. "One of them must be working with the Argents."

They heard a knock on the door of the cabin. Violet went to open it. It was Chakrit. "I saw the man," he said. "He ran and jumped in his van with the camera case and drove away very fast. He won't get far, though. I've already called the police and reported his license number. They will arrest him."

"He was also sneaking around in the elephant area," Benny said. "Can he get in trouble for that?"

Chakrit grew very angry at that news. "Yes, we will have him charged with trespassing too.

The Detour of the Elephants

If everyone is all right, I need to go check on the elephants. They will be upset someone was in their area."

"We are fine," Jessie said. "Thank you, Chakrit. At least we won't have to worry about him anymore."

Chakrit said good night and left. Everyone else sat down in the living room to talk about what to do next.

"It will be hard to pretend we don't suspect either one of them," Violet said.

Cousin Joe scratched his head. "I don't understand. Why wouldn't they just take the artifacts and give them to the Argents? Why is the person pretending to work for the Silvertons?"

"I've been thinking about that," Henry said. "If he gives himself away, he won't be able to arrange for anymore artifacts to be stolen from the Silvertons in the future. He will be kicked out of the Reddimus Society and arrested. Whoever it is wants to continue to fool the Silvertons so he can keep taking things that don't belong to him." He yawned. "I'm too tired to think of anymore plans tonight. Let's work on some tomorrow."

Everyone went to bed. The next morning, they visited the elephants again and then collected their things for the ride back to Bangkok.

Chakrit helped them load their bags into the taxi. "I received a call that the man has been arrested. You won't have any more trouble with him."

"Thank you again for all your help," Jessie said.

"You're welcome. If you ever come back to Thailand and want to learn how to care for elephants, we always have openings."

Benny and Soo Lee looked at each other. "How old do we have to be?" Benny asked.

Chakrit grinned. "Sixteen would be a good age."

"We won't be sixteen for a long time!" Soo Lee said.

"Don't worry," Chakrit said. "The elephants will still be here."

On the way back to Bangkok, Jessie said, "We'll have to find a time when we can talk to Trudy about all of this. I don't think she suspects either one of them."

"I don't either," Violet said. "She would have told us."

The Detour of the Elephants

"I still don't think it's Emilio," Benny said. "It just can't be."

Jessie checked her phone. "I've got a message from Trudy," she said. "She's arranged for a flight for Cousin Joe and Cousin Alice and Soo Lee back to the United States later this afternoon."

"We have to go on by ourselves?" Benny asked. He wasn't so sure he wanted to continue the Reddimus Society mission. The Argents scared him. He didn't like knowing Anna Argent might already be on her way to their next stop.

Cousin Alice put her arm around Benny and smiled. "There will be someone to meet you when you land at the next destination."

"Who?" Violet asked.

"It's a surprise," Cousin Joe said. "This has been quite an adventure, but Alice and I need to go back to work."

At the airport, Cousin Joe and Cousin Alice and Soo Lee walked with them to the terminal where the Reddimus plane was parked. They waited while the Aldens climbed on board and then waved good-bye. Emilio met the children on board. He was his usual self, laughing and making jokes. Henry began to wonder if Benny was right. If anyone was working for the Argents, it didn't seem like it could be Emilio.

"I'll miss them," Benny said, watching the cousins walk away.

"I will too," Jessie said. "But it will be exciting to see who meets us next."

Mr. Ganert came out of the cockpit. "We were worried," he snapped. "We were afraid all the artifacts had been lost. How could you fall for such a silly trick? Going all the way to Thailand? Someone did a good job of fooling you. I think I should talk to Mrs. Silverton about this. Clearly, we should get someone else to return the remaining artifacts."

"They're doing just fine," Emilio said. "Any of us could have fallen for that trick. And besides, they haven't lost an artifact yet. I'd say that means they should keep going."

"We're taking good care of them," Jessie said. "And we're all working together to keep them safe."

"Yes," Benny said. "Just like elephants. If we work together, we can do the job."

The Detour of the Elephants

Everyone but Mr. Ganert laughed. "You're right, Benny. We are good at working together."

"We have three artifacts left," Jessie said. "I wonder where we are going next."

"The answer may be here. I've got another package for you," Emilio said. "A messenger delivered it to us in Beijing." He took an oddly

shaped package out of a storage cabinet and handed it to Jessie.

"Benny, do you want to open this?" Jessie asked.

"Yes!" Benny said.

He ripped off the wrapping. Inside was a folded envelope and an angled piece of wood. The wood was decorated with a pattern of dots and lines on it.

"What is that?" Violet asked. "It kind of looks like an L, though the edges are curved."

"Or it could be part of a triangle," Benny said. "But it's missing a side."

"It's a boomerang," Henry said. "I have an idea of where we are going." He smiled. "This should be fun."

**Read on for a
sneak preview of**

THE SHACKLETON
SABOTAGE

**The fourth book of
the Boxcar Children
Great Adventure!**

The Aldens mission to return lost artifacts around
the world leads them Down Under, where they
must return an artifact to a dingo sanctuary!

"We should let you know that someone might try to steal the artifact," Henry told to Dr. Webb, the owner of the sanctuary. "There's a woman who works for a group called the Argents, who has been trying to take all the artifacts we're supposed to return. It's probably a good idea to return it to the museum as soon as you can."

"No worries, my friend!" said Dr. Webb with a smile. "Out here, there is nothing to worry about. The dingoes will bark if they see anything suspicious. Ha ha! They also bark if they see anything fun or exciting! Oh, and some of them bark when they're hungry."

"They're even barking right now," Violet said.

The dingoes were barking. It sounded like excitement and fun, the way Watch would bark when he saw Benny pick up his favorite tennis ball. He knew that meant it was time to play.

The sounds of the barking grew fainter, and Violet frowned.

"Doesn't it sound like they're going farther and farther from the yard?" she asked.

Dr. Webb tilted his head.

"Yes, it does a bit," he said. "Let's go see what's going on out there."

The Aldens went with Dr. Webb out to the yard, where they found all the dingoes were running around, *outside* the pen. Someone had opened the gate! Dr. Webb's assistant, Mimi, was holding one of the puppies and trying to call the others back to the pen, but the dingoes were having too much fun romping and running beyond the yard. Some of them thought Mimi was playing a game of tag with them.

"Dr. Webb!" cried Mimi. "You have to help me call the dingoes back! They might listen to you."

Dr. Webb rolled his sleeves up and nodded. He put a finger in his mouth and made a loud whistle. One of the dingoes came running back with his tail wagging, but the others were busy chewing on sticks and rolling in the grass.

"I guess we will have to do this the old-fashioned way! Violet, you and Benny stand near the gate. When the dingoes come back to the yard, open the gate for them, but then close it after so they don't get back out. Henry, Jessie, and I will go chase the others down. Mimi, would you get some of the special treats from inside?"

Mimi went to get the treats while Henry and Jessie trotted out of the pen. At least two dozen dingoes frolicked in the lightly wooded area outside the yard. It looked like all the dingoes were having a great time playing. A couple dingoes smelled the special treats and ran to Henry and Jessie when they called. After they came back into the yard, Violet and Benny gave them the treats for being well behaved. Then they carefully latched the gate so they couldn't escape again.

Some of the dingoes were more interested in playing tag with Dr. Webb. They wagged their tails and let him come close, but then ran away at the last second. Jessie could swear the dingoes had a sense of humor and were having fun teasing them.

Eventually, they managed to corral the dingoes

back into the pen. Dr. Webb counted them to make sure every one had been found.

Mimi locked the gate to make sure it would stay shut.

"I wonder who opened the gate," she said. "When the gate's come open before, it's been by accident because it wasn't latched all the way. But I know that I latched it properly today. It couldn't have opened by accident."

"And look at that," said Benny, pointing down at the path. There was a footprint in the dirt that didn't match the footprints left by the children, Dr. Webb, or Mimi. "Doesn't that look like a sneaker?"

It had taken at least half an hour to find all the dingoes and call them back to the yard. The gate might have been opened so that everyone would be busy finding the dingoes. No one would have been inside to keep an eye on things—including the box and the artifact.

The Aldens exchanged glances. They knew who might do such a thing. The same person who wore sneakers that matched the footprint by the gate...

The Boxcar Children
Is Now a Feature-Length Film!

With an all-star cast including Academy Award–winner JK Simmons, Academy Award–nominee Martin Sheen, and up-and-coming actors Zachary Gordon, Joey King, Mackenzie Foy, and Jadon Sand.

Available on DVD or VOD from your favorite retailer!

Love the first movie?
Look for *Surprise Island* coming fall 2017!

GERTRUDE CHANDLER WARNER discovered when she was teaching that many readers who like an exciting story could find no books that were both easy and fun to read. She decided to try to meet this need, and her first book, *The Boxcar Children*, quickly proved she had succeeded.

Miss Warner drew on her own experiences to write the mystery. As a child she spent hours watching trains go by on the tracks opposite her family home. She often dreamed about what it would be like to set up housekeeping in a caboose or freight car—the situation the Alden children find themselves in.

While the mystery element is central to each of Miss Warner's books, she never thought of them as strictly juvenile mysteries. She liked to stress the Aldens' independence and resourcefulness and their solid New England devotion to using up and making do. The Aldens go about most of their adventures with as little adult supervision as possible—something else that delights young readers.

Miss Warner lived in Putnam, Connecticut, until her death in 1979. During her lifetime, she received hundreds of letters from girls and boys telling her how much they liked her books.